Ever After

MIA SKYE

Edited by: Victoria Ellis of Cruel Ink Editing + Design

Cover Design by: Cady Verdiramo of Cruel Ink Editing + Design

Formatted by: Victoria Ellis of Cruel Ink Editing + Design

DEDICATION

To my husband who has always encouraged me to keep going.

Ever After

MIA SKYE

Mia Skye

PROLOGUE

MY HUSBAND AND I ARE SUPPOSED TO BE FIXING OUR MARRIAGE
while on this getaway, but instead, I needed time to clear my
head. Now that I'm in a better headspace, I head back to the
Hilton hotel where Aiden and I are staying. The place is beautiful but I'm alone. I square my shoulders, and maybe it's the
drinks talking, but I came here to solve our problems, not create
new ones. We've always said we are each other's *happily ever
after*. I can't give up now. I press the button for the elevator to
take me up. My anxious butterflies are coming back. The closer I
get, the stronger they get. I walk into the elevator and press the
button for floor twelve just as a family joins me. The quick,
upward motion of the elevator going up hits the pit of my stomach. The jolt isn't helping my anxiousness. Sensing someone
staring at me, I turn my attention from the floor and find a little
girl's wide-eyed stare on me. A smile stretches across her face,
and I feel the corners of my own lips turning upward as I give
her a slight wave just as the elevator signals that we've reached
my floor.

Once in front of the door, I swipe my card and disregard the
do not disturb sign. The door catches on something, and

confused, I push harder. A shuffling sound comes from the bedroom.

"Aiden, are you up?" I call out.

A gasp echoes in the room as I step over a shirt. Not a shirt... a dress. I pick it up and look at it. It's cheap polyester fabric and covered in pink leopard print—definitely not mine.

Am I in the wrong room?

I panic before seeing my black suitcase right by the closet where I left it. Drunk or not, I'd recognize that beat-up old suitcase anywhere.

My breaths turn shallow as I slowly walk toward the bedroom. Once there, my heart drops as I flick the light on. The room is spinning. Is this seriously happening right now? I'm grossly fixated on what's in front of me.

This definitely isn't what I was expecting.

Everything suddenly registers, alcohol swarming through my veins or not, the pieces all start to fall into place. I run over to Aiden just as he stands, and I slap him as hard as I can manage.

"What the fuck is this?" I scream. His eyebrows shoot up as all the color drains from his face. Before I can even fully comprehend what I'm doing, my palms are hitting his chest over and over, and screams are pouring from my chest. Tears run down my face before I can stop them.

"I didn't know he was married," the stupid bitch whispers. I look over at her.

"He's wearing a wedding ring!" I grab his hand and shove it in her face so she can see his ring better. She stares at me wide-eyed.

"Get the fuck out!" I yell.

She moves, but not fast enough. I grab her by the hair and drag her ass toward the door.

"What about my clothes?" She squeals as she tries to fight me off of her, but it's no use.

"You should have thought about that when you decided to sleep with my husband."

I shove her out the door. I don't fucking care if she walks out naked. Hopefully this teaches her a lesson.

Look for a damn wedding ring next time, lady.

I spin back around as Aiden walks up to me. He's put on some shorts. I don't know what to say so I just stand here. My head pounds as the room spins. It must be the alcohol and adrenaline mixing and forming a terrible cocktail inside of me. Aiden grabs my hand but I pull it away from him and stare in disbelief.

"I don't know what to say."

I'm going to pass out. There is a glass of water in front of me. My hands shake as I reach over and grab it. I raise the glass up to my mouth, spilling water all down my chin. I turn to Aiden. "Why would you do this? This is our trip to work on our marriage, and you're in bed with someone else?"

"I don't know what I was thinking. Everything happened so fast. I should have stopped it. I didn't think this would happen. Believe me," he says, pleading.

Is he serious right now? Who says that? "What the fuck? You sound as stupid as the bitch you stuck your dick in." He stays silent. "You didn't know what was happening. Did she roofie you or something? Doesn't look like it because you seem pretty coherent to me. Where the hell did you even meet her? We were apart for three to four hours at the most. You picked up a girl in that short of time. Is she a prostitute? Did you pay her?"

Shaking his head, he sighs. "No."

"Then how?" I yell, my tempter getting the best of me.

"I went to another bar, and we started talking. I was upset and slammed way too many shots. One thing led to another. It meant nothing. I love *you*. I always have and always will," he says, moving closer toward me.

I take a couple of steps back. "You *love* me? Really? Well, you have the worst way of showing it. We're here to help our marriage and instead of being present for me, you take your dick out and be present for some whore." I hope the neighbors aren't hearing anything from us. I can't stop yelling. He has to be kidding me with these lackluster responses. As I turn around to head out the door, Aiden grabs my hand. I stare at him dead in the eye, wishing my tears would dry up so I wouldn't give him the satisfaction.

"No, please don't go. I'll do anything to show you. This is something I want to work on. I'll even smash my phone because I know how much you hate it. Lilah, I love you. Please don't go!" he pleads.

"You should honestly just shut your mouth, Aiden. You are stupid as hell if you think I'm staying with you now. It has taken everything in me to work on this marriage. *Now* you want to break your phone and be present? Why weren't you present when I asked you to be? It had to take me finding you pounding another bitch to want to smash your phone." I pull my hand free from his and walk out the door. Aiden follows me out.

"Don't follow me!" I yell and he stops in his tracks, probably surprised I raised my voice in the hallway.

I really hope I don't run into the woman my husband just cheated on me with.

I could just yank her around by her hair this time.

My anger is so deep and intense that I'd probably do more.

CHAPTER ONE

TWELVE HOURS BEFORE

USUALLY WHEN I STEP FOOT INTO AN AIRPORT, MY TROUBLES leave me and the hustle of the place brings euphoria back into my life. My body and mind are more at ease knowing I'm leaving my troubles and responsibilities for the next week. This time feels different. As we both walk quietly side by side, that euphoria never comes and my troubles are still shadowing me. This time, as I propel one foot in front of the other, every muscle in my body contracts as my pulse quickens. I wipe the tiny beads of sweat forming along my brow as my stomach knots.

It's been hard getting along with my husband. We are at the point in our marriage where every little thing sparks an argument and blows up into something bigger than it should be. *The seven-year itch.* Our therapist suggested we take a trip to remind us of what we love about each other and try to bring our marriage back to life. Aiden and I agreed on Hawaii. I thought it would be a nice romantic place, and neither of us has been there. We both have been so busy with our lives that we forget about our marriage. There really isn't anyone to blame. It takes two to make a marriage work. But lately, I feel like I'm the glue that's keeping our marriage together. It's been exhausting...but I love my husband. So, I'm trying.

"Are we taking Delta?" he asks.

"Yes," I reply, heading toward the baggage check-in.

Once I get to the front desk and give the lady the confirmation number, I feel like we're finally making headway.

"Aiden and Lilah White," she confirms, then checks our bags in and hands us our tickets. I look over and see the security line is dreadfully long. I seriously hate this part. So does everyone else, I'm sure. I'm willing to bet no one of sound mind is excited about the long lines of the airport.

"I told you we should have applied to go through TSA. You never want to spend money," Aiden says with a sarcastic tone. I try my best to ignore his comment. Usually I would say something back but I don't have the energy. The internal stress and heartache are causing my head to throb. I don't want to make it worse.

Once we're finally in our seats on the plane, Aiden immediately pulls out his phone. I sometimes feel like I'm in a relationship with his phone *and* him. Our therapist gave us this long list of questions she suggested we ask each other to get to know one another again. We got married so young. She says it's common for couples who marry young to grow apart from one another but we can still make the marriage work despite us changing. We have to get to know each other again. Obviously, the questions are not happening right now. He's already in a salty mood so I pull out my book and read instead of angering him further.

I'm awoken by the rough plane landing just over four hours later. We make it through the airport in record time and pick up our vehicle—a lifted Jeep that Aiden and I have talked about purchasing for years ... we just have yet to pull the trigger. This will be a good test ride for us. For our marriage and the potential Jeep purchase.

Conversation between the two of us feels forced—and that's

if there's any at all. I'm thankful when I see the bright neon sign with palm trees telling us we've made it to the Waikiki Hilton. Scanning my eyes over our surroundings, I realize it's right on the beach, and I'm amazed at the rows and rows of balconies overlooking the glistening blue ocean.

"Are you hungry? We should go get dinner, I'm starving."

"Sure," Aiden agrees nonchalantly. "Where do you want to go?"

I pull out my phone to find a place to eat. Trying to find one we both agree on as we walk to our room. Aiden opens the door for me, waiting for me to go in first. At least he still has some manners toward me. We lay our suitcases down and both head to the bed to check out how comfortable it is.

I hand Aiden my phone. "Does the place look good to you?" I focus my attention on him, mesmerized by how attracted I still am to him after all these years. His beautiful blue eyes and soft light brown skin pair well together. I've always loved his milk chocolate brown hair. I tried to dye my hair like that before. It didn't turn out too well. My hair is way too dark and set in its color.

"Yeah, that place looks good."

"I'm going to shower really quick," I say as he hands me my phone back. Walking to the bathroom, I turn on some country music to ease my mind. A lot of my family members dislike country. They say it's way too sad. I don't know why, but it makes me feel better. Even the sad songs.

I don't worry about putting foundation on because it will melt away with all the humidity hanging in the air. I put on some mascara, eyeliner, and a bit of highlighter. Running the brush through my hair, I debate if I should put it up in a bun or not, because I already know it'll become frizzy. I throw some mouse in my hair and call it good, hoping Aiden thinks I look nice.

As I walk out of the bathroom, I see Aiden has changed into a tank top and shorts. He knows I like it when he wears tank tops that show off his biceps and tattoos. I'm a sucker for muscular arms and ink.

We arrive at the sushi restaurant we agreed on and order our drinks.

I ask Aiden, "Do you want to go through the questions the therapist gave us?" He shrugs his shoulders and I take the lead, pulling my phone out to start with the first question.

"What's something you used to believe in relationships but no longer do?" I ask.

"I used to believe that if you got married once, it would be your happily ever after." My heart beats faster, like it's going to jump out of my chest with how hard the palpitations are. I want to yell and scream at him. I try to stay calm. How could he say that?

"Are you referring to us?" I ask calmly.

"You can think of it however you'd like to."

"What do you mean? You are obviously talking about us. It's not like you've been married before."

"Like I said, think what you want. The therapist told us to be honest. If you can't handle my answer, then we shouldn't go through these."

He has a point. The therapist said that. But his answer still stings. Does he not feel anything? Sometimes I wish he would end the marriage himself and save us both the grief. I don't even feel like he loves me and wonder why he sticks around.

I was twenty when we met. A mutual friend had us over for a party. He was so cute. I kept staring at him, hoping he would come over and talk to me. I was hesitant to make the first move. After he caught me staring multiple times, he finally came over to talk to me. Throughout the night, he made sure to always be by my side. Brushing his shoulders against mine, always making sure I had a full cup to drink, offering his seat to me. It was the little things that made me feel giddy inside. He didn't want anyone else to talk to me, so he stuck by me. He was so adamant about us dating. I thought it was the liquor talking. We stayed up all night just talking and laughing. Once the sun came up, we knew we should part ways and get some sleep. It was hard for us to leave one another. Aiden asked for my number, but I didn't give it to him because I was trying to play hard to get. So young and naïve, I thought that was what men wanted. When he hugged me goodbye, I felt so safe and small in his arms. Like nothing could hurt me with the strength of his arms wrapped around me. It was a feeling unlike any I've ever had since.

I remember going home that morning so tired. I got to my room, threw off my clothes, went straight to my bed, and curled up into my blankets. As I was about to fall asleep, I heard a ping on my phone. I rolled over to get it off my nightstand, and there was a text message from a number I didn't know.

> Unknown: Goodnight. When will we see each other again?

My face lit up reading it. It was Aiden. I couldn't wait until the next time I could see his defined arms, bright eyes, and earnest expression. Every time I saw him after that, my stomach would flutter with butterflies.

The good times make me want to fight for us. I know we can get back to that place. I've seen so many marriages end too soon because when things get tough, no one wants to work it out. They call it quits before even trying to see if things *could* work out. Therapy is expensive. I can see why couples would try to work it out themselves before seeing a professional. Some even feel ashamed to go. I never felt that way. Aiden did. That's why it took us so long to see someone. He never thought we needed it. When he finally agreed to go, I was dumbstruck. I hurried and made an appointment that night before he changed his mind.

"Are you going to answer the question?" he asks, interrupting my thoughts.

"Yes, I'm not sure though. I know that it's a lot harder than I ever imagined."

I stop what I'm saying as the server comes over with our drinks and we order our food. Once she's gone, I go on to the next question.

"How am I doing as a wife?"

"Okay, I guess. You could give me more space."

My eyes go wide as I look at him. Did he really say that? "Are you fucking serious? This is one reason we are having problems. We give each other *too much* space. We are room-mates at this point. Do you not see this? Does this not bother you?" He looks at me, shocked, as if he said nothing wrong.

"You don't have to get pissed off."

"Pissed off? I don't understand. Do you even know why we took this trip?" I shake my head, feeling so dumbfounded.

"Yes, to work on our marriage."

"Why would you say you need more space? Haven't I been giving you enough space already? We hardly talk, we barely do anything as a couple anymore. You have your friends and I have mine. We both live separate lives. That isn't how a marriage should be."

He stays quiet.

"Do you not understand where I'm coming from?" I ask.

"Yes, I do," he says.

I don't know if he understands or if he is trying to get me to drop it. I debate if I should tell him what he could improve on, but I don't want this argument to drag out. There is an easier question that I scroll down to, hoping this will lighten the mood.

"What did you find most attractive about me when we first met?"

"Your eyes."

I smile.

"My eyes. Why?"

"They are big, brown, and beautiful."

My cheeks heat up. I wiggle around in my chair. After all these years, he still makes me bashful.

"What did you like about me?" he asks.

"I liked your arms." I laugh. Aiden gives me a questionable look. "What? They're muscular. I like muscular arms. But not any kind of muscular arms. The arms that are big and buff. Not muscular like chiseled out."

We laugh together. This is what I miss. Being playful with him. The server comes by and sets our food down. I order another drink and Aiden gets another beer. The alcohol is loosening both of us up. We haven't drank with each other in a while. When we drink together, we both get aroused. I'm wondering if that will happen. I don't even remember the last time we had good sex. It's always rushed or uncomfortable. We're not as comfortable with each other as we used to be. It makes me sad because I've noticed myself hiding from him.

"What's the next question?" he asks.

I scroll through the questions and find another playful one. For the trip, I will stick to easier questions. I don't want our trip to blow up.

"If you could travel anywhere outside the country, where would it be and why?"

"Hmmm. Probably Rome. It has a lot of history, and I would love to see the Colosseum."

"I would like to go to Greece. It looks beautiful. The houses that live on the sides of the mountains would be nice to look at and explore."

I throw my own question out there to see if he remembers. I ask, "What's my favorite color?" This should be a no-brainer, since everything I choose is pink.

"Pink," he says.

"And yours is black."

The server brings out the other rolls. We eat these in silence, which I'm okay with, and it doesn't seem to bother him.

CHAPTER TWO

AFTER DINNER, WE WALK AROUND THE SHOPPING AREAS THEY have in the Ala Moana Center. My body is more relaxed and at ease. It's probably the alcohol that's calming me. The wind helps with the humidity, too. It seems late because the sun has already gone down, but it's only around seven o'clock. Everyone is walking around and grabbing dinner. Some people are still in their swimsuits from their earlier visits to the beach.

There hasn't been much tension between Aiden and me since the restaurant. It feels good. We've been holding hands and going from store to store looking around. We are walking past a booth selling oysters with pearls in them when Aiden stops and pulls me toward the booth.

"Let's get you a pearl."

I look up at him and smile and follow him to the booth. The employee explains how it works. You pay to pick an oyster that holds a pearl in it. You can put the pearl in a ring, earrings, necklace, or bracelet. She let us know they are easy to set, and she could have it ready for us by tomorrow if we decide to set the pearl.

"Do you want to pick an oyster?"

"Yeah! This sounds fun." I walk over to the bucket of water to get the oysters. I turn to Aiden and say, "It's hard to choose. Do I pick a big oyster, small, or better looking shell?"

"I don't know. You could close your eyes and feel around and feel what one you like the best."

"Okay, here goes nothing." I close my eyes and feel around the oysters. Some feel smooth like a seashell and others are rougher around the edges. I chose a smooth one, and I open my eyes and my hand is holding one that doesn't look too bad. The employee asks if I want to open it but I ask her to do it. I don't want to risk losing it or damaging it. She opens it up, and it's a small pink pearl. "It's beautiful," I say.

"It's pink, your favorite color," Aiden says.

"Do you know what setting you want it in?" the girl asks.

"Yes. Let's get a necklace." I pick out a thin rose gold chain to put it on. She lets me know to pick it up tomorrow around this time. Aiden hands her his card and pays for it. As we walk away, I grab his hand and say, "Thank you."

"You're welcome. Anything for you."

"Do you want to get a drink?" I ask.

"Sure, that sounds good. The buzz from earlier has gone away, and this humidity is making me sweat, even with the wind. An air conditioned place sounds good right now," Aiden explains.

We stop at a bar to get some drinks. Music plays in the background as people chatter, talking and laughing and sipping on drinks. We grab a booth and I marvel at the air conditioning. It feels so good. The waiter comes over and takes our order. As soon as he leaves, I notice Aiden already on his phone.

We sit in silence as he thumbs away on his phone. I'm waiting to see how long it takes for Aiden to get off his phone. The night has been good so far. I don't want to ruin it with my nagging. The waiter brings us our drinks, and I chug mine. Before the waiter leaves, I ask for a shot of tequila. I might as well get tipsy if we're going to sit here in silence. I look around at everyone around me. Couples are laughing and talking together. Even the waitresses are laughing with the people in here. I sit here and wonder what people think of us. It's so disrespectful to be out with someone and sit on your phone. It is a common occurrence when we are out together. I stopped going out with him because of it.

My shot comes and I take it down quickly. The waiter sees I'm a little irritated. He takes my shot glass away and asks if I want another and I nod. Aiden looks up and gives me a questionable look and shakes his head.

"What?" I ask.

"Nothing. Wondering why you are pounding shots."

"You see nothing wrong here?" I ask and he looks at me with a confused look.

"Do you realize it's embarrassing to sit here with you while you sit on your phone the whole time?" I ask. I don't want this to trigger a bigger fight, but I also want him to be present with me.

"What's embarrassing about that?" he asks with his phone still in his hand.

"It's rude. You're ignoring me. Don't you see everyone else around us talking and laughing with each other?"

He looks around. "I don't care what other people are doing," he says with a shrug of his shoulders.

"Shouldn't you care about how it makes me feel? It *is* rude. You're not even present with me, you're present with your phone."

He stays silent, chugs his beer, pulls out his wallet, and throws a twenty on the table. Then, he glances around as if he's looking for the exit.

"What are you doing?"

"I'm going back to the hotel. I don't want to argue with you."

He stands and I immediately start to regret everything.

"You are going to ruin this trip for us. We are supposed to be working on our marriage," I say, while looking up at him. He's trying to leave me. This is embarrassing.

"That's why I'm walking away. I don't want to ruin this."

"By walking away, you are ruining it."

"I thought I was ruining it by being on my phone. You need to make up your mind." He turns his back toward me and walks out without another word.

I don't know what to say. He walks away as I watch, defeated. I want to burst into tears. Why do I keep putting myself through this? I keep trying over and over. I love him a lot and can't picture my life without him. Our marriage needs to go back to how it was when we first met. We were so happy. He always wanted to be with me. I always got butterflies when he would text me to go out somewhere. I sometimes still get butterflies, but not the giddy kind, more like an anxiety kind. Where you feel like something is going to explode because it usually does. Maybe that's PTSD from all our fights. Who knows at this point? I don't get where it all went wrong. I know we've been busy. All marriages are busy, though. Why can't we seem to work it out?

The waiter brings my shot and asks, "Do you think he will want another beer?"

"No. He had to go back to the hotel for work." The waiter nods before walking away.

Now I'm lying to not look so stupid for sitting here alone. Everyone looks happy as I look around. I wish I had that. I try so hard to hold my tears back. It's only nine o'clock now, and I would rather not go back to the hotel. The hotel is about twenty minutes away if I walk. I decide to just find a beach to walk on so I can cool off. I ask the waiter for the check and finish my drink. A little tipsy. It kind of helped take the edge off after everything, but this all still sucks.

Once I'm done paying, I walk toward the ocean. It's sad I'm doing this all alone. Hawaii is so beautiful. This is the first time we've been here, and we're both alone. Taking off my shoes and digging my toes into the sand, I sit here and watch the waves come up, then recede. The tension starts to be swept away with every wave that rolls back down. There is something relaxing about being alone right now. I should have just come here by myself.

Aiden pops back into my head. I can picture him sitting in the hotel room on his phone. I wonder what he even thinks. Does he feel sorry? Does he feel bad? He has to feel something. We are having a hard time, but he is a human that has feelings—at least he used to. Sometimes it seems like he has no feelings anymore. He at least agreed to go to therapy with me to work on our marriage. I was surprised, and it gave me a bit of hope. When he agreed to go to Hawaii, I was even more hopeful. He really wants it to work. But then again, who would turn down Hawaii? His actions are all over the place. He goes to therapy, comes on this trip to Hawaii. He answered some questions when we started at dinner. It was his idea to get me a pearl. He shows he cares and then he doesn't. That's what is making this so much harder. It's been so difficult to decide to leave because every time I feel like it's over, he shows up. Then it's good for a little while, and then he goes back to being so soulless. It's a roller coaster. A constant up and down, up and down. I'm surprised I don't have vertigo.

CHAPTER THREE

PRESENT

I FINALLY GET OUTSIDE. THANKFULLY, I DIDN'T RUN INTO HER walking naked through the hotel. God, I hope she was as mortified as I am by this entire situation. Looking around, I realize I didn't have much of a plan prior to storming off—I didn't exactly have much time. My phone is still charged, thankfully, and I glance at it to check the time. Almost midnight. My limbs are literally shaking from the adrenaline running through me. I walk along the sidewalk, trying to find a place to go. I have no idea how to feel. This is the last thing I ever expected from Aiden. Yeah, he can be a straight-up asshole sometimes, but I never expected *this*. I've always trusted him. He is never flirty around other women, never checks them out. Sure, he briefly looks, but doesn't everyone? It doesn't mean they are checking them out all the time. Even if he was, it was never to a level that made me uncomfortable. He doesn't even talk to other women. I know some of my friends have boyfriends and husbands that talk to women regularly. He's never done that. I don't understand what happened tonight. What made him do this? We have been through much worse, and I never thought he would go off to sleep with someone else. He usually stays home and blows off the steam there. Has he always been like this, and I was too oblivious to notice? I don't know what to think.

This has to be what it feels like to be in shock.

I'm surprised I'm not crying. But it feels like my emotions are all over the place. My attention is drawn to the music up ahead, and I walk toward it. I take a couple steps down and enter a bar. My body is suddenly hit with vibration from the live band playing. It's not overly loud but enough to counteract the adrenaline running through me. Many people are dancing and sitting in the back closer to the band. There is a bar in front of me where a few people are sitting. I bypass the bar and head for the bathroom. I don't look that bad in the mirror. My skin glows from the humidity. I grab a tissue and wipe the mascara under my eyes that has now caked to my skin. Returning to the bar, I take a seat. The corner is taken by another guy, so I can't sit there. Opting to slide onto a stool a few seats down, I do my best to turn my frown into a smile when the bartender asks what he can get for me.

"Shot of tequila and a mojito, please," I say, needing to feel the comfort of my go-to order.

As I sit and focus more on the music, I notice it's more of a county-rock vibe. Hopefully Aiden won't find me, if he's even looking for me. The bartender sets my order down in front of me. Handing him my card I ask, "Can you open a tab for me?" He reaches for my card as he gives me a smile and walks to the cash register.

I guess the guy next to me is alone, too. No one sits by him. I don't dare look over and attempt to give off the worst vibes I have ever given. I'm in no position to talk to anyone. Through the corner of my eye, I notice him staring over at me...unless I'm seeing things wrong through my peripheral vision. My eyes are all cloudy from the tears.

What am I going to do? I'm supposed to be here for an entire week. I'm going to have to get another room. The waiter comes back, and I ask for another shot. God, I hope I control myself or I'll end up sleeping on the streets. Right away, I take another shot. I still feel like this guy is staring at me. I finally look over as he gets up and walks away. Guess he's leaving. Sliding off my chair, I move over to the corner chair and position my back to sit up against the wall. I sip my drink, still wondering what the hell I'm going to do. I pull my phone out and look for other hotels to go to.

I lose all concentration with everything around me. I hear someone pull out the chair next to me and sit. My heart drops. This better not be Aiden. I don't want to look up. I'm getting the feeling of the room spinning. *Please don't be Aiden, please don't be Aiden.*

The guy who was sitting here before is the one I look up at. "I'm so sorry I took your chair." Sliding off my chair, I say, "I thought you left." Heat rises to my cheeks and I like an idiot, but I'm thankful it wasn't Aiden.

"It's okay. You don't have to move. I'll sit here." He points to the chair next to me.

"Are you sure?"

"Yes."

"Thanks for the seat." I slump down in the chair, still scrolling on my phone. Everything is so expensive at the last minute. I don't know where to stay that'll eliminate the chance of running into Aiden. There are a lot of other cities I can go to and stay in. Why should I be doing this? Aiden is the one who put us into this mess. He should have to find somewhere else to stay. I can't even stand to talk to him right now to tell him to leave the room. The more I look, the more frustrated I get. I slam my phone down. Images of Aiden and that girl run through my mind on repeat. I feel the guy staring at me, so I meet his eyes.

"What are you staring at?"

He looks a little taken aback. "Sorry, I just... are you okay? I'm Jay, by the way."

Despite not being in the mood to start a conversation with a stranger, I did take his seat. I mutter, "I'm Lilah."

"Beautiful name." He grins, and I can't help but notice he has an amazing smile. It makes me angry. I should hate all men right now. I should hate all of their stupid smiles. I give him a slight smile and look back at the live band that is on the stage playing.

A few minutes pass by, and I still notice him staring at me. I turn and look over at him. "Can I help you?" I ask, getting more annoyed.

He clears his voice and asks, "Are you waiting for your husband? I can move over?"

I squint my eyebrows, confused. "No." Why would he ask that?

"Did you travel alone to Hawaii?" he asks.

Hesitant to answer, I say "No." Now this is really getting weird. Is he a human trafficker? No, he wouldn't be a human trafficker picking someone up in a well-established place. I should leave. This is the last thing I need.

"I was wondering because I see you're wearing a wedding ring," he says, looking down at my left hand that is laying on my lap.

Why is he even asking these questions? I pull my wedding ring off and throw it in my purse. I don't want to wear this thing. It represents nothing it's supposed to represent.

"I came here with my husband, but about an hour ago I walked in on him fucking someone else in our hotel room." I gasp. Oh god, why did I blurt that out? "I'm sorry. I don't know why I blurted that out." He's going to think I'm fucking crazy.

He looks over at me with a concerned look. "Don't be sorry. That's a hard situation. I couldn't imagine coming here and finding my wife doing that. Are you okay?"

"Honestly, I think I'm in shock right now. Not sure what to think or do. I left all my stuff in the hotel room and came here.

You don't want to hear this on your vacation. I'm sorry. Ugh. Sorry. I don't know why I keep saying sorry."

He lets out a quick chuckle. "You don't have to be sorry for anything. I understand some of what you're going through. I'm supposed to be here with my now ex-fiancée. This was supposed to be our honeymoon trip."

Now I feel even worse that I've been such a bitch to him. He's going through a hard time too. "Oh really? What happened? I mean, you don't have to tell me if you don't want to. It's none of my business." I want to put my head in my hands and forget any of this is happening.

"The day of our wedding, I found out she was sleeping with one of my best friends. He was a groomsman in our wedding."

My eyes grow wide. "That's awful."

"It is. I wish I found out sooner. After all the money we spent on the wedding and this honeymoon…well, it would've saved me a lot."

I try to take a sip of my drink, but realize I'm out.

"Do you want another drink?" he asks, motioning to my empty glass.

"Yes, thank you. This is going to be a long night. Might as well enjoy it." I shouldn't have more shots at this point. I'm getting pretty drunk. Jay asks the waiter for another mojito for me, and as he's asking the waiter, I realize how handsome he is. He has dark brown hair, brown eyes, and a nice tan on him. Both of his arms have tattooed sleeves on them. He's dressed very simple, in a black T-shirt and shorts and some white sneakers.

I'm pulled out of my thoughts when I feel my phone vibrate. I grab it off the table. "Shit," I mumble to myself. It's Aiden. I turn my phone off and shove it in my purse. Fuck him, he can worry for once.

"So, if you came to your honeymoon, did your ex come, too?" I question.

He finishes the last gulp of his beer and looks over at me. "No. This was going to be a surprise. She didn't know about it."

This honeymoon was to surprise her, and she gave him the worst surprise instead. How can people treat their significant others like this? I look over at him as he twirls his empty beer bottle in circles.

"Did you come alone, then?"

"Yes, I wanted a trip to myself after everything. I thought maybe it'd clear my mind."

"I get that. I was thinking of leaving and going back home, but why should I? I'm already here." I shrug. "When did you get here?"

He shifts his body toward me, almost touching my knees. "I got here last Saturday. I'm here for another week. You?"

"Today."

"Today?" he asks, shocked. "How the hell did your douchebag husband find someone on the first day here?"

I'm still trying to figure that one out myself. "I honestly don't know. Our therapist suggested this trip to help us rebuild our marriage. We've been having a hard time. We went to a bar to have some drinks and ended up in an argument. He walked away, and a few hours later I went back to the hotel…you know the rest. A lot of good this trip did. Now I'll be filing for divorce when I get home."

"You don't want to work it out?"

"No! He knows that this is something I would never tolerate. Cheating is a hard limit for me. Did you try to work it out with your ex?"

"No." He laughs. "She and my supposed friend can live happily ever after with their fucked-up situation. He was a married man with children. I had to break the news to his wife that day, too. Eventually, my ex is going to realize how bad she messed up. There's no way she'll want to be a stepmom or deal with the kids' mom."

The waiter sets both of our drinks down and takes our empty cups away. "Did they stay together, then?"

"I don't know. No one tells me and I don't care to know."

"You sound like you're pretty over it already?"

He shrugs his shoulders. "It's been six months. I had to move this trip out after everything went down. We had bought a house that we were going to move into, but I sold it and bought another house. It's been a crazy six months. I'm still hurt. Especially knowing that it was one of my best friends, but…it is what it is." He looks down at the bar before back at me again, and I can see the hurt flash in his eyes. It isn't something you can just get over quickly.

It makes me wonder where I'll be six months from now.

Will I still feel this betrayed?

"I'm so glad Aiden and I don't own a house. This divorce would be even messier than I can imagine. When does this bar close?"

"Two o'clock, I think."

I reach into my purse and grab my phone, checking the time. I forgot I turned it off. "Do you know what time it is?"

He taps on his phone that's set down on the table to brighten it up. "It's almost that time."

Nerves hit the pit of my stomach. Where the hell am I going to sleep?

"Do you want to walk down by the beach?" he asks.

"Sure, I need to run to the bathroom first, though," I tell him as I get up from my chair.

"If you're not coming back, let me know. My feelings won't be hurt." He laughs.

I laugh. "Shut up. I'll be back. Plus, I have nowhere to go. A walk will be nice." I shrug my shoulders and walk over to the bathroom.

As I start the walk, I realize I'm a little more intoxicated than I thought. I shouldn't have agreed to go to the beach when I need to look for a hotel. I get to the bathroom and look at myself in the mirror. "What a mess," I say, to no one but own reflection. My cheeks are bright as a tomato from the alcohol. They pair well with my red eyes. As I walk back to the bar, Jay is getting up from the chair, asking if I'm ready to go. "I need to pay first," I say.

"Don't worry about it, I covered your tab." He puts his wallet back into his back pocket and the bartender hands me my card.

"You shouldn't have. I should have covered yours since I stole your chair."

He laughs and leads us outside.

The humid air hits my skin, and I feel a little at ease. I don't know if that's because I'm not alone right now or if it's because I'm in Hawaii. I never expected to feel this calm. When I'm calm about unpleasant situations, I know I've accepted it. Should I have accepted this situation this soon? Have I accepted it because deep down I knew it wouldn't work and I needed an out? Why couldn't I have been strong enough to leave Aiden before this?

I needed something to finally push me over the edge. I still don't know how it is going to be when I get home. There is still an entire process I will have to go through. Who knows what will happen between now and then? I wish I could run away and not deal with it—or him.

"Are you okay? You look deep in thought?" Jay asks.

"Yeah, I'm thinking about what I'm going to do now." We got to the beach and found a spot to sit. I kick off my sandals and run my feet and hands through the sand. I'm calm because of where I'm at. When I arrived at the beach earlier tonight, I was calm. I'm calm now again.

Jay is taking off his sneakers and asks, "Are you going to stay in Hawaii and finish out your vacation?"

"I want to, but I need to find another hotel and get all my stuff. I don't want to go back there and see Aiden."

"I'm assuming Aiden is your husband?

"Yes." I pull my legs up to my chest, and rest my chin on my knees as I look out into the ocean.

"Does he know where you're at, or has he tried to call?"

Out of the corner of my eye, I see Jay leaning back on his elbows with his legs straight out in front of him.

"He called a little bit ago while we were talking, but I didn't pick up and I turned off my phone. I was worried he would come looking for me. I'm glad he hasn't."

"Good," he says. "Let him worry."

"I don't even know if he is worried or not."

"He should be. Never know who you might meet while strolling around." He gives me a wink.

A shy smile spreads across my face. We've just barely met, but I'm comfortable around him. One of those comfortable feelings where it seems as if you've known each other forever. I feel like I can tell him anything and he understands me. Sadly, we have so much in common with our love lives. I know nothing about him aside from that, but still. His presence is comforting, and it's making this terrible night better.

"So, where do you live?" I ask.

"Texas."

"Is that where you were born?"

"No, I moved around a lot when I was a young. My parents settled down in Texas, and then I was placed into foster care. I hardly remember my parents. At sixteen, I emancipated myself so I could get out of the foster care system."

"That must have been rough."

"It was. I have a really close friend named Alex. His parents took me in until I graduated high school."

"That was nice of them. Do you have any siblings?"

"Not that I know of. I lost contact with my parents when they put me in foster care. From my understanding the court ordered them to either find a family to take care of me or I would have to go to foster care. They ran everyone they knew out of their lives. They made their living by stealing, from what I've heard. I don't really know or remember," he says and shrugs his shoulders. "What about you? Any siblings?"

"Nope. Just me and my mom. Dad walked out on us when I was young, and I never really cared to ask about him. All I know is he was in the army and had to always pick up and leave. Since they weren't married she couldn't go with him, and I don't think she wanted to go with him anyway," I admit.

"Where are you from?" he asks.

I always get weary of telling people where I'm from. Many people think of Utah differently than it really is. "Utah."

"Are you Mormon?"

Of course he asked that. "Hell no." I laugh. "And if I was?"

He laughs. "I don't know. I thought I would ask. Isn't that the state capital of Mormons?"

"Yes. Utah is a weird state but it's also surrounded by beautiful mountains. The mountains and beautiful scenery make up for what we have to deal with for calling it home," I say, trying to change the subject so I'm not reminded about the one particular person I have to deal with. "What do you do for a living?"

"I'm a contractor for commercial buildings. What about you?"

"I'm a nurse but I currently work remotely under a provider that has his private practice and specializes in telehealth." He gives me a questionable look. "I do most everything a nurse in a conventional office does, like ordering tests, prescriptions and following up with patients on how their treatments are going. Stuff like that, but everything is all over the phone."

We sit in comfortable silence for a bit as the wind picks back up and the waves crash against the shore. It's nice not thinking about Aiden. Not thinking about everything that needs to be sorted out. I just sit and I let the silence continue to calm me.

Once the two of us have been in our own worlds for a bit, I decide to pick back up the conversation between us.

"So Jay, do you have a last name?"

"It's Hart."

"Jay Heart," I repeat. "Like heart the organ?" I say as I point to my chest.

"Without the E."

"That's cute, I like it," I say with a smile.

Jay starts to laugh. "Not until you know where I got it from?" I raise my eyebrows wondering what he means.

"When I was born my parents were using alias names. So Hart isn't even their real last name."

"Really?" I ask, shocked. "How do you know so much if you never knew them?"

"The foster care kept records of everything the courts had on my parents. When I emancipated myself they gave me all the information they had and I did some digging of my own, too."

Our conversations turn into jokes and laughter for the rest of the night. We both decide to get into the water. I don't have a swimsuit on, so I go in my clothes. I can't help but stare at Jay as he takes off his shirt. His broad chest and tattooed arms make my knees go weak.

"Ready?" he asks.

I hurry and turn away from him so he doesn't notice me staring.

"Yes, let's go."

Once my feet hit the water, I pick up the pace and run. He runs after me, and I sense him right behind me. His hands grab my waist and make me pause. He picks me up like I'm a baby being cradled, and I wrap my arms around his neck and hold on. He runs deeper into the water. "No!" I scream and laugh, but just as I get the word out, he dunks both of us under. I come up for air while still in his arms. I notice I'm straddling him at this point. We are both staring at each other, and he leans in. I'm getting nervous. My cheeks are heating up. They are probably as red as an over-ripe tomato now. Is he going to kiss me? Instead, he hugs me a little tighter and rests his head on my shoulder. I feel my tension release. It's such a heartwarming gesture that I haven't received for such a long time. I haven't even known this guy for that long, but I feel an instant connection to him. Like a sense of familiarity with him like I've known him from another lifetime. It's hard to explain. I wonder if he feels the same or if I'm just reading into things...

The sun starts to rise, and Jay lifts his head and looks at me.

"We should go get some rest. We've been up all night."

"We should." I release myself from him. We walked back to shore to where we left our shoes. We are both soaked with no towels. I pick up my shoes and purse, and we head back toward the city together.

My mind spins because I'm not sure what to do at this point. I don't want to leave him, but he might think I'm using him. He *is* fun to be around, and I can finally relax and be myself. I always feel so tense around Aiden. It's like walking on eggshells with him because I never know what mood he is in or what will set him off.

"What hotel are you staying at? Maybe I can find a room there," I say.

"The Marriott," he says, drying himself off with his shirt.

Thank God he didn't say Hilton.

"Why don't you stay with me? It's late...well, I guess it's early." He laughs. "You've had a long night. I'll help you look for a hotel once we get some rest." I'd actually love that, but still...I don't want to invade his space.

"No, I don't want to intrude. I probably already ruined your night with all my drama," I say anxiously because I kind of don't want to be alone right now, but I also don't want to sound like I don't.

"You didn't ruin my night. I've been here for a week and

haven't talked to anyone. It was nice to have some conversation," he says.

"You haven't talked or met anyone else? I don't believe that. Why?"

"I don't know. I haven't found anyone I cared to start a conversation with." He looks over at me. "But I guess you set me up to start a conversation with you by stealing my seat." We both laugh.

I continue walking with him because I don't exactly have another option but also because I want to. The streets are quiet this early in the morning. A lot of early morning risers are walking over to the beach with coffee in hand. Some are already in swimsuits, too.

"I told you that was an accident. You don't know how stupid I felt."

He shakes his head and laughs. "I noticed you before you stole my seat. I wanted to talk to you but didn't know how to start a conversation. You looked deep in thought, and then I saw your ring."

"Really? What made you decide to talk to me then?"

"I don't know. When you sat down, I felt something. I don't know what it was or how to explain it. You looked happy and sad all at the same time. I guess I wanted to figure it out."

What if I stay with him and he thinks I'll sleep with him? I'm not in the right state of mind to do that. I'm not even in the right state of mind to even be spending time with someone let alone think about being intimate with someone.

"If I stay with you, you better not expect sex because I'm not—"

"Do you think that's what I want?" he asks, cutting me off.

"Isn't that what every guy wants?"

"Not me." He shakes his head at me. "I mean, sure you're beautiful, and I would have a hard time saying no if you came on to me. Trust me though, I respect women more than that," he explains. "I'd genuinely like to help you sort this out once you get some rest."

"Are you going to think badly of me if I stay over, given the situation I'm in now?"

"Not at all. I've been where you are. What helped me most was keeping my mind busy and hanging out with friends. I hope I kept your mind busy tonight. I was trying to, anyway."

My heart drops a little. He doesn't even know me, and he cared enough to hang out with me, so I would forget about what Aiden did.

"Are you okay?" he asks.

"Yes, I'm surprised, I guess. I didn't know that's what you were doing. It was nice of you, Jay." The cold from the AC sends a shiver rolling through me as we enter his hotel. The lobby is empty apart from the woman at the front desk.

"Do you want to stay with me or would you be more comfortable if we ask about getting your own space?"

"I'll stay with you. I need some clothes anyway." Looking down at myself. "I guess yours will do," I say jokingly.

He laughs and shakes his head. "Already stealing my clothes."

"What can I say?"

Once we get to his room, he opens the door for me. I walk in, surprised at how clean it is. The floor is spotless. The only thing sitting on the ground is his suitcase. Usually, my clothes are all over the place; he's clearly tidier than I am. Walking over to the balcony, I set my purse down and gaze out at the ocean. It's so beautiful with the morning sun shining down on it. I glance below us and see the pool. There are only a few people out swimming laps for their morning workout. The sunrise is lighting up the sky even more now. Sunrises and sunsets always put me in a good mood.

I turn around and ask, "Do you mind if I take a shower?"

"No, go ahead. My T-shirts will be a little long if you want to wear one of those." He hands me one of his black T-shirts.

I reach over and grab it from him. "That'll work."

Once I'm in the bathroom, I undress. My bra and underwear are still soaking wet. There's no way I can put them on after I shower. I didn't think about this part. This is going to be awkward.

I step out of the shower and grab the towel hanging off the towel rack. I dry myself off and throw on Jay's T-shirt, feeling bare in front of a stranger without my bra and underwear. I open the door and find Jay making himself a bed on the floor.

"What are you doing?" I ask.

"Making a bed for myself."

I walk over closer to him. "No, I should sleep on the floor. I'm putting you out way too much tonight. I can't let you do that."

"It's fine. You can take the bed," he says. "Really, I don't mind."

"We both need rest. Why don't we both sleep in the bed? I'm sure it will be fine. We are both adults." He gives me a questionable look.

"Are you sure?"

"Yes. It's fine. I'll put a pillow between us."

He grabs the pillow and blankets he had on the floor and throws them on the bed.

"I'm going to take a shower. Take whatever side you want." He walks off and shuts the bathroom door. I take the side of the bed farthest away from the room door. This is the spot I always choose. I feel safe when the man is closest to the door.

CHAPTER FOUR

THE SOUND OF JAY CLOSING THE ROOM DOOR STARTLES ME OUT of my sleep. Jay is walking in with trays of food in his hand, and my stomach starts to growl.

"Good morning. Hungry?" he asks.

Still reeling from the night before, I swing my legs over the bed, confused at what I've done. I went back to this guy's hotel without even knowing him. He could be a murderer for all I know. If he was though, wouldn't I be dead by now? Most likely. The alcohol and adrenaline from last night made me not think clearly. Luckily it turned out okay.

"Yeah, actually. I could go for some food." I look over at the alarm clock on the nightstand. It's one in the afternoon. I knocked out last night. I don't remember Jay getting into bed after he went to take a shower.

Then the realization hits, I have no clothes, and no place to stay after this. Sickness hits my stomach just thinking about going back to that hotel room to get my clothes. My eyes are fixed at the table as I sit down. Taking a plate, I serve myself pancakes he's offering. Jay lays a bunch of topping out in front of me. Taking some bananas and strawberries, I top my pancakes with them.

"I wasn't sure what you liked, so I grabbed a lot of choices," he states.

"You did good. I'm not a picky eater. I like everything."

"Did you sleep well?" Jay asks.

"Yes, I don't even remember falling asleep or you getting into bed." I push around my food. I was hungry a second ago. The sickness in my stomach made it disappear.

"What's wrong?"

"I'm feeling sick to my stomach just thinking about seeing him and grabbing my clothes." I wrap my arms around my stomach.

"Why don't you stay with me for the next week? We both could use the company."

That sounds better than staying here alone. Am I crazy about doing this?

"You wouldn't mind?" I ask.

"No. I enjoy your company."

Knowing I won't be alone in this beautiful place helps the tension in my stomach subside. I slowly release my arms around from my midsection and sit up a little taller. My clothes, how am I going to get them? I don't want Aiden to know I'm staying here. He might stay and try to follow me.

As Jay eats his eggs, I look over at him. "I'm going to go get my clothes. If I tell Aiden I'm leaving back home, I don't think he'll try to stay. I don't know how I'll go get my clothes without him following me around after I leave, though. I expect him to do that."

"Would he follow you after what he did?"

"I think he might, yeah. After seeing my face, the look on his was devastating." I reach over and grab some eggs to eat.

"I've seen that face before. The devastation makes little sense when they are the ones who betrayed us and got caught."

I agree and try to come up with a plan. I need to get my clothes and leave as fast as I can without him being able to follow me. I could really use a car. While walking with a suitcase, there's no way I can get away fast enough. He'll know if I'm not in a car.

"Do you mind if I borrow your phone? I want to make sure Aiden doesn't suspect I'm lying and trying to stay, I want to see what flights there are to go home. I know he'll stay if he knows I'm staying, and it'll ruin what's left of my trip if I run into him. I still haven't turned on my phone." Jay pulls his phone out of his pocket and hands it to me. Using the internet, I search for information. There is a flight flying out tonight at eight o'clock. I'll tell Aiden I'm leaving on that one. By the time he knows I'm leaving, it would be too late for him to get on the flight. I'm praying he just leaves and I can pretend none of this is happening for the next week.

"There is a flight leaving tonight at eight. I could tell him I'm getting on that one. Do you have a rental car by chance?" I ask.

"Yep, sure do."

"I need a car to leave quickly. He might follow me, and I won't be fast enough walking while dragging a suitcase."

"You need a car anyway if he's going to believe you're going to the airport. I should go with you."

"Who will you say you are?" I reach over and pour myself some orange juice.

"Just tell him I'm your Uber driver. At least I'll be there if he tries to stop you."

That's a good idea. "Is this all too much for you? I feel like I'm a stray dog you found on the street and you feel obligated to take care of me." I let out a sad chuckle and try to make the best of it, but I still feel bad.

He laughs along with me, his laugh a bit more cheery than mine.

"I understand your situation. Stop overthinking it. After today, you'll be able to relax more and enjoy your vacation."

It's now around four o'clock in the afternoon, and we're standing by the elevator waiting for it to open to get on. The elevator comes up, and we both step in and press the *L* button for the lobby. The second the elevator drops, so does my stomach. I don't want to see Aiden. Nausea rolls through my stomach.

The second we pulled up to the Hilton, I let out a sigh.

"Don't let him get to you. Get your stuff and come right out. I'll be here waiting."

I look over at Jay and smile. "Thanks for doing all this. You sure you'll be here when I get back?" I attempt a smile.

He rolls his eyes at me. "Yes. I won't leave." He taps his hand on my legs as a sweet gesture. Butterflies form in my stomach. I don't know if it's the nerves from having to see Aiden or because of his hand on my leg. I like to think it's because of Jay.

Once I reach the room, my nausea amplifies as my body and mind remember what happened here less than twenty-four hours ago. It felt like it took years to get up here. I slide my key in and open the door, and immediately there's a shuffling noise in front of me. I look up and Aiden gets up from the bed and rushes over to me. He tries to hug me but I'm not having any of that.

"Get off," I say as I push him away.

"Where have you been? I've been worried sick!"

"Good for you. Why didn't you worry when you brought trash to the hotel?" I walk over to the bathroom and grab my bag with my toilettes in it. Good thing I unpacked nothing but this. It makes it easier to get in and out quickly.

"I said I was sorry. Did you listen to my voicemails or read any of my texts? I've been trying to reach you and explain."

Aiden is following me around like a little puppy. I bend down, open up my suitcase, and throw my bag in it before righting it and grabbing the handle. Aiden stands right in front of me as I look up. Giving myself more space between us, I take a few steps back.

"I don't care what you have to say. Nothing you can say will make me believe you or forgive you. Save it for the next person who wastes their life on you." I walk away with my suitcase rolling behind me.

"Where are you going?" he asks.

"Home."

"When?"

"My flight leaves tonight at eight o'clock."

"Why didn't you tell me?"

His stupidity is driving me insane. He's apparently lost all of his brain cells. Was I too stupid to see he's been like this the whole time? I turn around and face him. "Why would I let you know? You're the last person I want to see. When you get home, please do me a favor and move out. It's the least you can do while we go through a divorce."

"Divorce?" he yells and walks back and forth with his hands on his head. "I thought we would work this out, Lilah. You're going to throw this away? What happened to working on things?"

My hands tremble. I'm trying to stay calm. I don't want him to see he is getting a reaction out of me.

"You thought wrong. I was happy to work on our marriage before you screwed someone else. Now I'm done. Everything I've tried was a waste of my time. You're done wasting my time and money. We wasted money on the therapist and now on this trip. I am done."

Aiden walks over to me and tries to pull me into a hug. I push him off and start walking toward the door.

"We can still work this out. I promise I'll change, and I'll even throw my phone away. I'll pay attention to you. Don't walk out on me. I know I'm a piece of shit, but everyone deserves a second chance."

I stop dead in my tracks and turn to him. "You think you haven't had second, third, fourth, and fifth chances this whole relationship? You've had many chances, and I was still here trying to work it out because I *loved* you. We always said we were each other's happily ever after. We even engraved it onto our rings." I open my purse and pull my wedding ring out and throw it at him. "I don't know when everything went wrong, but at least I know, deep down inside, I tried my hardest. That's more than you can ever say for yourself."

His face was stunned. I took off my ring. He holds it in his hand, looking down at it. "I tried my hardest. When you wanted to go for therapy, I went with you. I came on this trip. What does that tell you? I was trying."

"You think just showing up makes a relationship work? It takes more than just showing up to make a marriage work." As I get to the hallway, I calm my voice. I don't need a bigger scene. I go up to the elevator and press the down button. Aiden is right on my heels every step of the way. The elevator door finally opens what seems like an eternity later. I walk in and turn around to press the button to the lobby, and Aiden is standing right there in front of me. Oh great, he is going to follow me outside. Good thing Jay has a car. Without one, there's no way I could escape him.

The elevator door opens, and Aiden walks out first. He holds the door open for me, and I look at him and roll my eyes.

I pause a moment and take a deep breath before walking through the lobby, trying not to bring any attention to us. So many people are walking around and checking in. Aiden is still right behind me. I get outside to Jay's car with Aiden still on my heels. Jay must see me because the trunk pops open, and he gets out of his car. Oh no, what is he doing? My eyes go wide as he approaches me.

"Do you need help with your bag?" Jay asks.

"Yeah. Thanks." I thought he would stay in the car. Do uber drivers help people with their bags?

"Who is this?" Aiden asks, staring at Jay with a smug look on his face.

"An Uber driver," I say sternly, watching Aiden give Jay a dirty look. "How else do you think I'm going to get to the airport? Walk?"

"I would've taken you. We could have gone together."

"No thanks." I shake my head at him, making it clear I don't need his help.

Jay is back in the car when I look over. The door to the back seat is open. I don't know how real it would look if I got in the passenger seat. Aiden grabs my door before I can shut it.

"How am I going to get home?" he questions.

"I don't know. Try your hardest." He looks at me, baffled. I shut my door and Jay drives off.

While Jay drives back to his hotel, I rest my head and look out the window. My clammy hands stop sweating and shaking. It's easier for me to relax now.

We haven't spoken a word since we left the Hilton. I've been lying on the bed thinking and processing everything when I feel the bed dip in a little. Jay lays down next to me. Both of us look up at the ceiling.

"Do you want to talk about it?" he asks quietly.

"It's hard for me to know what to say or how to process it. There are still a lot of things I am trying to process." I'm trying to figure out if Aiden has always been this stupid, and I was just too blind to notice it. You always hear how love blinds you. Am I one of those people? "He thought we would try to work it out."

Jay turns to me with raised eyebrows. "Lindsee thought the same."

"Who?"

"Lindsee. My ex. That is her name."

"Oh." I guess I never asked what her name was. Unless I

forgot. I was pretty intoxicated last night. "Did you ever feel like love blinded you?" I turn my body over to the side facing Jay and place my hands under my head as if they were a pillow.

"Yes, love gets the best of us. Why do you ask?"

"Just everything that has happened. I wonder if it's been going on all along, and I was too blind to see it because I wanted to see the best of him and us together. He thought we would work it out and was stunned when I told him no. Has, he been that stupid all along and I never saw it? He thought he deserved a second chance…it blows my mind. In his head, he doesn't think I've already given him chances."

I'm embarrassed just talking about this to Jay. I never wanted to be one of those girls who was so blinded by love. Was it even love? Maybe we stayed with each other for so long out of comfort.

"It shows their lack of respect for the other person. I was blinded by Lindsee, too. When I look back at our relationship, there were times I should have questioned. It gets the best of us when we least expect it."

"I want to run away and not go back home and deal with everything. How did you get through it?"

"Time. Give yourself time. Work on it each day, keep yourself busy, and do what's best for you. Eventually, time will pass you by, and you realize how much you've overcome. When you're there in the moment, you think your whole life has ended. You wonder how you will ever go forward. Being with someone for so long, you become one person in a way. You both grow together. When it all comes shattering down, you feel you lost the other half of yourself. Then time goes by, and you realize you're not the same person anymore. It makes you stronger, more than you ever thought you could be," Jay explains.

I can't see why anyone would cheat on him. He's so sweet. He doesn't have to be wasting his vacation on me, but he keeps sticking around. Maybe he feels sorry for me. I hope he's not doing this out of pity. It is nice to have someone to talk to that has been through this. It doesn't make me feel as naïve. I wasn't the only one blinded. Love gets the best of us.

I need to tell my mom what's going on. I haven't spoken to her since we landed yesterday. I get up from the bed. "I should call my mom and at least let her know a little about what's going on. If Aiden goes home and I'm not there, he's going to be calling her. She will freak out and worry."

"That's probably a good idea."

Sliding the door behind me, I step onto the balcony. I sit on the chair in the corner and wait for my phone to turn on. I hate this. Resting my head back, I think about what I'm going to say. Once my phone is on, I'm flooded with text messages and voice-mails from Aiden. He texted me and called me at all hours of the night and day. I decide not to waste my time on them.

I call my mom and explain everything to her. She thinks I'm not in the right state of mind to be staying here alone. I assure her I'll be fine and will be at the beach most of the time relaxing. I promised her I won't do anything that could get me kidnapped or hurt. Mothers…all they do is worry.

After hanging up, a ping sounds from my phone. I look down, and it's another message from Aiden.

> Aiden: Please let me know when you get home. I worried about you all night and day.

I swipe through some of Aiden's messages, and it's the same old *I'm worried about you* bullshit. He's not worried about me. Clicking on my best friend Lia's name, I decide to text her.

> Me: Lia! Guess what?

> Lia: You're pregnant!

> Me: What? No. Why would you think that?

Lia: Why else were you going to Hawaii other than to jump Aiden's bones?

Me: Haha. Oh god, Lia, you knew why we came, and plus…even if I did jump Aiden's bones I wouldn't be pregnant this quick. We've been here a day.

Lia: Oh right! What's up then?

Me: Long story short: Aiden cheated on me on our vacation. I met another guy last night, and I decided to stay with him for the rest of the week. If Aiden contacts you, just ignore him please.

Lia: What the fuck! Lilah. What the hell happened? Are you okay? Why are you texting me instead of calling me about this?

Me: Yes, surprisingly I'm okay so far. The guy I met is named Jay and he's been keeping my mind busy so I don't dwell over all of this. I'm outside on the balcony and he's waiting for me inside. I didn't want to keep him waiting, that's why I didn't call you.

Lia: I'm going to kill Aiden. And you, too, for telling me this over a text message.

Me: Just ignore Aiden for now. I promise I'll make it up to you.

Lia: Are you sure you trust this new guy?

Me: Yes. We have this instant connection that's hard to explain. But I feel really comfortable around him already. Like I've known him all my life.

Lia: Are you saying you have a sixth sense?

Me: Shut up. Just trust me on this.

Lia: Okay I will. I guess go have fun with your new lover boy. Muah!

Me: Muah!

CHAPTER FIVE

"WHAT DO YOU WANT TO DO WHILE WE'RE IN HAWAII?" JAY asks.

I lay my head back on the lounge chair and spread my legs out in front of me. The sun beating down on my skin feels good. We're out by the hotel pool. I've had a few Piña coladas so far and feel a nice relaxing buzz. I don't know what it is about relaxing on the poolside doing nothing but people watching makes vacations worth it. Aiden was never one to relax. Come to think of it, this is my first time doing this. Vacations have always been go, go, go. This feels different, and I'm enjoying it more than I thought I would.

"I don't know. I had a lot of plans at one point, but now that went all out the window."

"We can still do what you wanted to do. Don't let what happened stop you."

"Honestly, it's nice sitting here and relaxing, knowing you have no plans and can do whatever you feel like at the moment."

"I'm up for anything if you want to do something."

"What have you been doing this past week?"

He lifts both his arms and says, "You're pretty much looking at it."

"You have done nothing all week?"

"I've explored a few places, but I guess I feel like you. Once I got here and started relaxing, it felt nice not having any plans."

Our waiter steps in front of us and asks, "Do you guys want another drink?"

I raise my empty glass toward him. "Yes, please. I'll have another."

He turns his head and faces Jay. "Anything for you, sir?"

"I'll have another IPA."

"Any food for you two?"

I turn to face Jay to see what he thinks. He shrugs his shoulders and says, "Do you have a menu we could look at?"

"Certainly. I'll bring that right out."

I wonder what Jay thinks of me because all I've done around him is drink. I was drunk when I stayed the first night with him. Who stays with someone the first day they meet and on vacation? But it's no different from hooking up with someone the first day you meet, followed by the walk of shame. All those girls have survived. My excuse was all the adrenaline and alcohol from that night. He didn't end up killing me. So that was a plus. I guess nothing else could get as bad as what happened a few days ago. Unless he ends up killing me…

"Here is your drink, miss?" the waiter says and hands me my drink.

"Thank you."

"For you, sir. Here are the menus. Let me know if you want to order anything?"

I pull my sunglasses off and scan the menu for something to eat. I spot a guacamole burger that sounds appetizing right now.

"Do guys care what a girl eats?" I ask.

It's been forever since I've dated. I don't know if I should pig out right in front of him or not. Wait. Why do I care? This will go nowhere.

He looks over at me with scrunched eyebrows and shakes his head. "No. Why?"

"Because this guac burger they have sounds good."

"Why would I care if you eat a burger?"

"I will end up looking like a pig because of it."

"Trust me, men don't care. And if they do, run, because that tells you they're shallow and only care about your looks or how you make them look."

I'm glad I asked. That's good to know when I date again. *Dating.* I can't even think about doing that all over again. It seems like so much work to go through the whole getting to know one another and trying to impress them. I don't even know how to date anymore. It's been so long.

We've been sitting here in silence ever since we finished our food. We were both clearly hungry, because we devoured our food.

"Have you dated anyone else since your ex?" I ask. That's the best I could do to start a conversation. I think to myself.

Jay laughs and says, "No, between work, canceling everything from the wedding, and buying a new house, I haven't even had time to think about dating. That's why I decided to keep this trip. To have some time for myself to relax and chill."

"Is she still with your friend?"

"I don't even know. I kind of knew something was going to happen to our relationship, but I kept pushing it along."

"That's how I felt. I kept waiting for our problems to get better, but they never did."

"Yeah, I know what you mean."

"Have you ever wanted kids?" I ask.

"Yeah, I do. One day. What about you?"

"I do, but maybe just one."

"Same. Kids are a lot of work."

"They are. I have some friends that had them at a young age. It changes your life. I think that's why I've waited."

"You're still young, though."

"I know I am, but living in Utah, if you don't have kids by the time you're twenty-one, you're an old maid."

"Twenty-one," he says, his mouth open and eyes wide.

"Yup."

"Your life is barely starting at that age."

"It has to do a lot with the Mormon culture over there. They turn eighteen, graduate high school, get married, and start a family. Some people that aren't Mormon fall into that, too. There was a high school teacher that I ran into. I think I was nineteen, and he asked me if I was married with kids yet. The shock on his face looked like I told him I killed someone when I said no."

"That's crazy. How did you not fall into that?"

"Watching them made me not want to fall into that. I got married young. That would be the only thing I fell into. Kids are on a whole other level. I didn't want to bring into the mix being that young. A few of my friends had kids at a young age, and watching how hard it was on them, made me want to wait."

"How old were you when you got married?"

"Twenty-two."

"Did you guys ever talk about kids?"

"We did and we never wanted them at the time. Then our problems came, and we both knew kids couldn't be in the picture. Did you and your ex talk about kids?"

"Briefly, I would always change the subject. Deep down, I'm not sure what I was thinking about the whole marriage thing. Every time subject of children came up, I would run from it. You live and you learn. Sometimes I think it is a blessing that she cheated on me. I just wish it wasn't with a friend of mine," he says and shrugs his shoulders.

I'm glad I stayed with Jay. He's fun and helps me take my mind off of things. I was dwelling on my marriage and trying to do everything the therapist told us to do. That's all my life was about for too long.

CHAPTER SIX

LIGHT SHINES STRAIGHT INTO MY EYES, MAKING MY HEAD THROB harder than it already is and wakes me up. I toss a pillow over my head to shield the light, but then in the distance, I hear clinking noises. The covers on the bed fall off as I lift my head and body to see where the noise is coming from. That's when I look down and notice I'm still in my swimsuit from yesterday.

"Good morning."

I lift myself up more and look over at Jay setting up breakfast on the table. My head is throbbing worse than before, and I lay my head back down on my hands and close my eyes.

"Do you have a hangover?"

My head barely nods.

"Want any breakfast?"

The second I hear those words, my hands come up to my mouth, stopping the vomit that's about to protrude out. I throw the covers off of me and rush to the bathroom.

After about ten minutes, I'm able to lift my head off the toilet. I start the shower and get in to scrub off yesterday's sunscreen and sweat. The steam from the hot water is helping the pressure ease off my head.

I'm trying to rewind my brain to yesterday to see if there is anything I did to make myself look stupid. I can remember how I got to our room. He didn't carry me back. At least I could walk.

I stumble my way out of the bathroom to the table in a robe.

"Do you feel better?" he asks.

"Better than before. My brain is still thumping against my skull."

"Eat some breakfast."

I reach over and grab a bagel and spread strawberry cream cheese on it. There are so many options he always outdoes himself.

"You should let me pay for our meals since you're paying for the room."

"I already paid for the room. It makes no difference to me if you stayed with me or not, since I had plans to stay here already."

"I know, but you even paid for the food and drinks yesterday. I don't want you to feel like I'm bumming off of you. And I'm sure you didn't have plans to pay for an extra person."

He curls his lips inward and looks at me and says, "I had plans for an extra person."

"Oh, that's right. At least let me pay for some dinners then."

"Okay, deal. What are you up for today?"

I turn my head, looking at the bed.

"You want to go back to bed?" he asks.

"Sort of," I say in a hushed voice. He's going to regret asking me to stay with him. "What time is it, anyway?"

"About six in the morning."

"Six in the morning! What the hell are we doing up?"

"You passed out after we went back to the room around eight last night. I fell asleep too."

"I'm sorry if I'm ruining your time."

"You're not. You're giving me more company than I had all week."

After my long five-hour nap, Jay and I decide to go to the Turtle Beach, which is on the North Shore. When I woke up, Jay was lying in bed next to me on his phone. He waited all morning for me to wake up. I thought we could check out another beach since I didn't want to be boring. When I searched Google, the Turtle Beach came up as a beach to see.

As we are approaching the beach, I hear a little girl's voice squeal in happiness at the sight of the turtles. I focus my gaze on her as she bounces lightly in place.

The turtles are surrounded by a rope railing, preventing anyone from approaching them. A person from a wildlife organization is speaking to a crowd about respecting turtles and not getting too close to them.

"Oh wow, they're bigger than I expected," I say.

A few turtles are sleeping in their shell, and it makes them look like big rocks. There is another floating in the ocean. I look over to my left and see one making his way out of the water toward the beach. The turtle flops down onto the sand like he's exhausted.

My grin comes up from my lips that reach ear to ear.

"Did you like the turtles?" Jay asks.

"Yes, they're cute. The little girl's reactions made it better."

We find a little spot on the beach and lay our towels down. We stopped at a gift shop to buy ourselves inflatable donut floats. Thankfully, the gift shop blew them up for us because I wouldn't have been able to do it.

"Are you ready?" Jay asks.

We get up and head to the water.

We're both holding each other's hands and resting our heads

back on the tube as we move in sync with the waves. The waves keep splitting us apart, and I finally grab onto his hand to keep us together.

It feels different being here with someone else other than Aiden. Aiden is the only guy I've spent time with since we started dating. Not being around him was something I needed to clear my head and understand what I needed…given he pushed us apart. All the tension I was holding onto for us to work out was causing me to make choices that weren't the best. I never realized how much it was dragging me down by holding onto him and the idea of what we could be again.

"What are you thinking about?" Jay asks.

"A little bit of everything."

"Do you want to talk about it?"

"It's weird because I thought I would be more hurt and heart-broken after finding Aiden with someone else. But I feel more relaxed. It's hard to explain, but I think all the tension we had was making it hard for me to see what it was doing to me and making it hard to make decisions that benefit me rather than us. Our entire relationship, I always made things about us—never about what I needed. Getting married so young didn't help either. I was still growing up and finding myself, but since I was married, I was finding myself while incorporating him. It made it hard."

"I get you. So far, do you feel good about your decision to divorce?"

"I do. I really do."

Jay turns his head over to me and catches my attention. We both smile at each other. My cheeks are warming up and it's not from the sun, it's from his cute smile that's making me bashful.

"Do you travel a lot?" he asks.

"Kind of. I try to do a couple of trips a year to keep me sane, but I haven't done much traveling the past few years."

"Maybe we can change that," he says with a wink.

"I'm up for it. And I promise I won't bring all my drama with me." I chuckle. "Where should we go next?"

"I'm up for Spain."

"Oh, Espana." I try to speak with a Spanish accent. "I'll have to brush up on my Spanish. Do you speak any other languages?"

"I learned Spanish in high school, just the basics, but lost it since I don't use it."

"We'll have to buy Rosetta Stone," I say.

The waves are picking up, moving us more. I squeeze Jay's hand a little tighter to keep us from drifting apart.

The next thing I know, I'm coming up for air. A gigantic wave came through and knocked us out of our tubes. I reach up and wipe my hair and water out of my eyes, searching for Jay. The waves keep coming in hard and knocking me down. I'm trying to get to the shore, but the waves are making it hard for me to balance.

I finally see Jay up ahead, running toward me. I'm immediately confused. Why is he running? I scan the beach to see if anything is happening, but everyone is enjoying their time playing in the water or laying out on the sand. The closer I get to Jay, the faster he's running up to me. My pace slows a little. I look over at a group of guys staring at me, and one guy hit his buddy in the arm and points my way. I turn and look behind me to see if there is something there, but there's nothing. My gaze shifts back over to the group of guys and, in an instant, I'm wrapped up in Jay's arms.

"I'm okay," I say. What the hell is going on?

"Lilah."

"Yes. What's going on? Why were those guys staring and pointing at me?"

Jay looks over his shoulder and says, "They're not looking anymore."

"Okay, but what were they looking at? And why are you hugging me so tight?"

"Lilah, you lost your top."

"What!" I say in a high pitched voice. I look down and he's right. My chest is bare. "Oh, my god. How embarrassing."

"What do you want me to do? I can get your towel and bring it to you or we can both try to walk together?"

"No, don't let me go. Let's walk together."

Jay walks backward, still holding me in his arms. At least he's a lot bigger than me. He huddles over me and can cover my front sides.

"I'm sure making your life interesting."

He chuckles a little. "You sure are. Don't be embarrassed, though. Shit happens," he says as he plants a kiss on the top of my head.

The kiss makes my body melt more into his hold. His touch makes me feel protected, and he makes me feel a lot better about myself than I have in a while.

CHAPTER SEVEN

JAY HAS BEEN GREAT TO ME THESE PAST FEW DAYS. HE'S DOING his best to make sure I'm making the most out of my trip. My mood has lightened up not having to worry about what I say, so it doesn't spark an argument. I never realized how much I walked on eggshells around Aiden just to make sure I didn't set him off.

We are at the beach relaxing, and I'm waiting for my phone to power on to check in with my mom. I promised her I would check in every day. The second my phone turns on, it goes off with text messages and voicemails from Aiden. It's been like this every day. I ignore them. I text my mom every day, letting her know everything is fine. Before I turn my phone back off, I wait for a response.

"I'm getting hot. Do you want to get in the water for a little?" Jay asks.

"You go ahead. I'm waiting to hear from my mom."

Jay gives me a wink and heads for the water. I look over at him walking to the beach, checking out his physique. He has muscles that pop when not even trying. The more I get to know him, the more attracted I am to him. He is very handsome. Every day I spend with him, the attraction increases. It doesn't help that we have some flirtatious going on from time to time—it's hard to ignore the feelings that are building for him. Sometimes I feel guilty because my marriage is still in the back of my mind while I'm having these thoughts. Sometimes I think I should go home so I don't start something with someone else. Jay reassures me he understands my situation, but he doesn't understand the attraction I have for him and why I should go home.

The ping of my phone interrupts my thoughts of Jay. My mom texted me back. I reply, letting her know I'm turning my phone back off and I'll text her again tomorrow. I get up from my towel and fix my swimsuit bottoms, so I don't have a wedgie walking to the water. Jay's back is facing me as I step into the water. I get a thought to jump on his back in one of those flirty ways, but I haven't dared to do anything like that. Even though the first night we met, he was holding me and hugging me while in the water. I never thought I would see him again after that, so I didn't care and wasn't shy. The liquor that night gave me courage, too. Instead, I walk right next to him.

"Glad you could join me."

I give Jay a slight smile.

"Everything okay?" he asks.

No. Every damn day my attraction for you grows. It's becoming harder to hold myself off of you, and I don't know if I should be even feeling this way.

"Yep." I turn to Jay and smile again. "It's getting close to dinner. Do you know what you would want to eat? I'm getting hungry."

"Anything sounds good. Let's head back to the hotel and get ready."

Every time we have to shower, Jay always lets me shower first. He's giving me a lot of privacy. Sharing a hotel room with a stranger hasn't been so bad with him. He jumps in the shower while I'm in the room changing so I can have my privacy. Sometimes I wish he'd just make a move though, so I can get this attraction or whatever this is over with. I don't want to be the first one to make the move. What would he think of me while married? What should I think of him wanting to do something with a married woman? I throw the thoughts out of my head and wrap the towel around my body before heading out of the bathroom to change. Jay barely looks at me while I'm naked under a towel. He heads for the shower and shuts the door.

I roll my eyes, then drop my towel and start imagining him coming up behind me and touching me softly. Kissing me on my neck. Running his hands up and down my torso. Wanting him to grab my boobs and play with my nipples instead, he brushes his hands gently around my boobs, teasing me. I feel desire pooling at my center. I imagine myself reaching back to grab hold of his cock. Feeling it pulsing in my hand, I run my palm up and down his shaft. He's so big and thick. It makes me even more wet. I run my hand down to my clit and touch it, my breathing becoming heavier.

The noise of the door opening startles me, ripping me from the daydream.

"Oh shit, I thought you would be dressed by now. I'm so sorry," Jay says in a nervous voice.

In a state of utter panic, I search for my towel. As soon as I grab it, I cover myself up. *Holy shit.* Did he see anything? I was so deep in my thoughts I didn't even hear the shower turn off. My face is growing hot. Not wanting to look at him, I keep my head down.

"It's okay. I got lost in thought. That's all," I say stuttering. I walk over to my suitcase and start looking for something to wear. Jay is still standing there. "You don't need to go back to the bathroom. I'll grab something and dress there." I turn around and start heading for the bathroom. Jay is still standing in the same spot.

"What were you doing?" he asks, his voice lowered and husky, vastly different than I've heard from him.

"Nothing." He clearly saw me playing with myself. My face grows hot again.

"If you need some private time, let me know."

Oh fuck. I don't know how to get out of this. Come to think of it, I don't even know when the last time I had sex was. No wonder I'm getting wet over my damn imaginations.

"Can we act like you saw nothing?"

"There's nothing to be embarrassed about. It is human nature to masturbate."

Did he have to say masturbate?

I don't want to masturbate. I want you to fuck me!

That's why I'm embarrassed.

I don't know how he feels about me sexually, and I'm over here fantasizing about him and then he catches me. Good thing he can't read my thoughts.

"Well, in that case, I'll let you know the next time I need private time." I laugh, playing this off.

After walking into the bathroom and shutting the door, I lean against the door, trying to catch my breath. Wow, this trip is getting better and better. I keep making a fool out of myself. No wonder he keeps me around. I'm great entertainment for him.

We get to the restaurant, and I avoid looking at Jay as much as I can. He brings nothing up. Why can't I be mature about this? We've both been a little quieter than usual. I'm waiting for the server to bring my drink so the alcohol can ease my nerves.

It's so beautiful here, sitting outside on the patio overlooking the ocean. I wish I could get out of my thoughts and just enjoy this moment...but my mind refuses to let earlier go.

It feels like a lifetime passed when our drinks finally come. I take a big sip and feel the warmth rush down to my stomach. I look over at Jay and break the silence. "Does Lindsee still reach out to you?" I ask. That's what I think to bring up to break the silence? Nice Lilah, nice.

"Yes, she still does from time to time. It's her begging for forgiveness and admitting she messed up. She misses me. Blah blah blah. I ignore her most of the time."

If they have no more ties keeping them together, why hasn't he blocked her out of his life? I wish I could do that with Aiden. We're still married, though, and have joint everything pretty much. Just more to think about splitting up...

"Why haven't you blocked her out of your life completely?"

"There was still a lot we have to talk about. Like the house and accounts we had together. I guess by the time that was all done, I was over it and didn't feel the need to block her out. She doesn't get to me anymore. Not like she used to."

The server brings our food and we both ask for another drink. I look over at the sky and the sun is setting and lighting up the sky in pink hues. My body has eased up after what happened earlier. My eyes meet Jay's and I smile. I don't know where I would be if he wasn't here. I hope he doesn't feel like I'm using him as a rebound. He has said he understands what was happening and knows I need someone. That someone is your best friend, though not the opposite sex and someone you just met.

"I appreciate everything you have done for me. Not sure

where I would be or what would have happened if I didn't meet you. Please don't feel like a rebound," I say.

"I know you're not using me as a rebound. It's best to have someone there for you when stuff like this happens. I couldn't have done it without my friends. I know our situation isn't normal, but who cares? There are no rules of what is right or wrong in this kind of situation."

Jay makes a good point. There are no set rules. Our situation is out of the norm. That's what makes this easier.

Having drank a little too much, both of us are wobbly as we walk back to the hotel. Our bodies keep bumping into each other while walking and laughing about nonsense. When we realize we took a wrong turn, halfway down an alley, we stop and stare around, totally confused. I don't think either of us kept track of how much we drank.

"I can't believe we didn't realize we were going the wrong way," I say. Jay's as confused as I am. "Have you ever gone this way before? Does it go to the hotel?"

"No, I don't think so. We should turn around before we get more lost."

As we turn around, I lose my balance and grab onto Jay's hand to help steady me. I pulled him in with me against the wall. My back hits the wall and catches my balance. We are now face to face. Jay put his arm above my head, catching himself. I look up at him and he rests his head against his arm. We end up locking eyes. My whole body stiffens and grows warm. Sweat is building up my body. He stares into my eyes. I can't swallow at this point. Every time I do, my throat is making a huge gulping noise. This is even better than my fantasy I had of him earlier. I feel his warm breath on me. It's making me even more warm inside. He rests his other hand up against the wall next to my head before moving in a little closer. His forehead is resting against mine now, and my pulse starts to race as tension between us builds. I lift my head a little more to get closer to his lips. He moves his head and places a long kiss on my forehead. Disappointment hits me. I turn my head and say, "We should head back." We both turn back the way we came and head back to the hotel in silence.

CHAPTER EIGHT

WE DECIDED TO DO THE LANIKAI PILLBOX HIKE IN KAILUA. JAY
has been leaving everything up to me with what we do. I haven't
felt like doing much. I'm a little disappointed in myself for not
feeling up for it. Hawaii is a beautiful state, and all we've done is
eat and lounge around. That is enjoyable too, but I had plans and
places I wanted to go with Aiden that were ruined. I haven't felt
like doing those plans anymore. After all the food and lounging
around we've been doing, my body feels awful. I feel bad for
Jay, but he keeps saying it's fine, and he's enjoying himself.

Since all I've done is eat, I wanted to move my body. After a
friend recommended this hike to me, I brought it up to Jay, and
he was all for it. I'm sure he's sick of eating and lounging around
but he's too nice to say anything.

We pull over and park once the GPS lets us know we are
here. We didn't consider the locals' commute to work when we
checked how long it would take to get to the hike. The drive
ended up being three hours because of an accident.

I slide out of the car and feel the heat beating down on my
skin.

"Are you ready?" Jay asks.

I nod my head. It's already hot, and I'm dreading my decision to go on this hike. Jay seemed into it though, and he's been so nice to me, letting me choose everything we do and places we eat. I decide to just stop being a baby and go.

After about ten minutes of silence Jay asks, "Do you hike a lot?"

I've been trying to stay quiet so he won't hear my huffing and puffing, especially since we are going uphill; I sound like a smoker trying to catch a breath on a regular day.

"I used too," I say with a shallow breath. "I used to be more active but the older I got the less active I became. It's a shame because I'm feeling it now." I stop in my tracks and take a huge breath of air. "This is embarrassing."

"It's okay. We can take as many breaks as you need, seriously."

"No, I'm not embarrassed of stopping. I'm embarrassed that I have to stop. My endurance is horrible. I need to get back into shape. This hike is only thirty minutes up and thirty minutes down. We've only walked ten minutes so far."

Jay reaches out for my hand and pulls me along. "Will this help?"

"Yes, but won't you be embarrassed you have to drag me up here?"

"I don't care what people think."

My small hand feels like a baby dolls hand in his. It's actually comforting how small I am compared to him—it's like he can always protect me.

After what feels like another twenty minutes of us hiking, I check my phone and realize it's only been five. I ask Jay, "Do you do anything active? I mean, clearly you must. You're in great shape." My cheeks grow warm and I shake my head at my awkwardness.

"I'm on my feet a lot already with work so that does keep me pretty active. When I have time, I like to hit the gym."

We finally make it to the top of the mountain. There is this cement-looking box with graffiti all over it. Now I see why they call it a pillbox. I guess you could consider this a pillbox. I read on Google that it used to be military bunkers.

Jay steps up onto the box and reaches his hand out to mine. "Grab my hand." I reach my hand up, and he pulls me up like I weigh nothing. After I steady myself, I look out. I gasp at how beautiful it is. You can see the rocks in the blue water. There are so many people in the ocean, but up here they look like tiny ants. We walk over to the edge and hang our feet off the sides. The breeze up here feels nice.

"This is beautiful," I say to Jay. I'm in awe right now. I turn to Jay and ask, "Is this your first time in Hawaii?"

"Yes. Is it yours?"

"Yes. I never expected it to be so breathtaking. I knew it was beautiful, but not like this." I grab my phone and take a few pictures. The ocean is in the background as I take a selfie, and it makes me happy that I'll get to remember this moment every time I look at the photo.

"Jay, get in this one?" He doesn't hesitate and turns around. I snap a few of us together. Stupid Aiden is missing out. This would have been perfect to rekindle our marriage. I get a sick feeling in my stomach thinking about it. My emotions are everywhere once again. One minute I'm fine, then I'm pissed, and then sick. Jay must sense how I'm feeling because he wraps his arm around me.

"Are you okay?" he asks.

I look at him and smile. "Yes, just thinking." There is a silent pause before Jay speaks again.

"If there is anything you want to talk about, I'm here." He must have thought I would say more. He knows not to push; he's never made me talk when I haven't wanted to.

An hour passes by, and we head back down. We both allow silence to linger between us as we walk, and it isn't ever even a little uncomfortable. Jay gives me the space I need to think. I did little thinking because I was worried about slipping down the hill. Downhill is easier to walk than uphill, but it's also easier to slip.

Once we get back to the car, we head over to check out Lanikai Beach, which the hike overlooked. The neighborhood we drive through to get there is beautiful. Trees and bushes surround the houses, making it more secluded and somehow even more alluring.

As we walk down to the beach, the sun is setting, and families are packing up to go. A lot of couples are standing on the beach and watching the sunset together. Some are sitting on blankets with a bottle of wine and hors d'oeuvres. It's super romantic. It makes me happy for them to be in that place of their relationship, even if I'm a little sad for myself—and for Jay, too.

"I should have been a little more romantic, huh," Jay says. He's probably seeing all the couples together as well.

Laughing I say, "No, it's okay, it's not like you're trying to be with me." We stop and find a spot and sit down.

"Maybe I am."

My heart beats faster and the hairs on my skin stick up with goosebumps. I don't know what to say to that. Silence spread across my lips. What *can* I say? I don't even look at him. I sit and stare out at the ocean in silence while trying to gather my thoughts.

CHAPTER NINE

NATURAL LIGHT SHINES THROUGH THE CRACKS OF THE BLINDS the next morning. I'm lying on my side, and there is a heaviness wrapping around my waist. Still half asleep, I move my ass a little back to see what it is. I bump into something hard. What could that be? I rotate my hips in circles, trying to figure out what that hard thing is. The heaviness around my waist pulls me closer. I open my eyes a little, but the sleepiness takes over and my eyes shut again. The hard thing behind me moves in circles now, matching my movements. My ass and hips are moving in sync with this thing. My breathing becomes a little heavier. I'm getting turned on. Why am I getting turned on? I hear breathing behind me get a little heavier. My clit is pulsing, aching to be touched. I drag one of my hands down to my clit and start a circular motion. The circular motions behind me speed up. I'm having a wet dream. This is how wet dreams feel? They feel like the real thing.

I open my eyes a little more and look around in front of me. The light from the day is shining right at me. I'm a little more coherent now, and I freeze. I swear it feels like both my heart and breathing stop. My circular motions end on impulse, and the heaviness around my waist is Jay's arm wrapped around me. He's spooning me. The hard thing behind my ass is his cock. *Holy shit! He's having a wet dream.* We were having one together. I stay still, unsure of what to do. Do I stop him or let him finish? If I let him finish, he will be so embarrassed. He'll be embarrassed either way. I know I am. How would I stop him, though? He'll wake up if I move as if I'm still asleep. I rack my mind, contemplating what to do. Then suddenly, every inch of him stiffens and the motions stop. Did he finish or wake up? I felt nothing wet.

I turn around to look at him, and I see his eyes wide, like I caught him robbing a bank. Jay pulls his arm off me and lies on his back.

"Were you awake this whole time?" he says.

"Kind of." He has his arm over his eyes as I look over at him. I contemplate if I should tell him I was doing the same thing before I woke up, so he's not the only one embarrassed. I was the one who was caught fantasizing about him and touching myself. What more can I do to humiliate myself? At least he doesn't know it was him I was fantasizing about.

I reach over to take his arm down from his face. "Jay. Don't be embarrassed." He cuts me off before I can finish.

"This is embarrassing. I'm sorry. I can't believe that happened. It's never happened before." That makes me feel better. I'm the first person he's done this to. He's the first person I've done this to. We have so much sexual tension built up for each other it was bound to happen sometime.

"I was doing the same thing to you when I woke up and realized." Jay turns his head toward me and looks at me. I turn to look over at him. I can't help but laugh. We both don't know how to act in this moment. Should I crack a joke to end the silence?

"If you want some private time, just let me know. There is no shame about masturbating." He cracks up laughing and throws his arm over his face again.

"Touché," he says, laughing shyly.

It's our last night in Hawaii, and we both have early flights. While we pack our stuff, we stay in and order room service. We haven't spoken about where we go from here. We've both been unusually quiet today. I'm assuming it's because neither of us knows how to bring up going back to normal life. I'm happy Jay asked me to stay with him. I don't know what I would have done if I were here alone; I probably would've just moped around and felt sorry for myself.

"How are you feeling with everything, knowing you're about to go home?" Jays asks.

"I don't want to face all of this. I know I have to, but it would be nice for more time to pretend like none of this is really happening." This past week flew by so fast. It's been nice being with Jay. It has lifted some weight off my shoulders while being here. I guess you never know how much someone is dragging you down until they're not around anymore. Things happen for a reason. This is something I had to go through to realize how unhappy I've been.

"I'm glad we met and spent this time together. It's been a huge eye-opener for how unhappy I've been."

"If you were this unhappy, why didn't you leave him before?" Jay asks.

"We've been together so long I thought it was normal to go through these phases. We both let too much time go by, and by the time I tried to fix things, it was too late to get us back." I zip up my suitcase and walk over to the bed and sit down. Jay continues packing. I sit up and rest against the headboard. "I got married so young and everyone told me to wait. They said I was too young to make this decision. Part of me feels like I didn't want to prove everyone right," I say.

Jay stops packing for a moment and looks at me. "Don't

blame yourself for it not working out. If you felt like it was the right thing to do, then it was for yourself or both of you."

I shake my head and agree with him. It is something I felt was right. I shouldn't let everyone else's opinion get to me.

What's going to happen when I get home? Will Aiden be there? I told him not to be. What is going to happen with me and Jay? Are we still going to talk? There is chemistry between us, but we have said nothing about it. I don't want to lose contact with him, but does he feel the same? I don't want to ask. How is that going to look on me? Well, I guess at this point it doesn't matter. I stayed with a man for a week that I didn't even know.

Jay comes and sits on the bed in front of me and clears his throat. I look up at him, confused.

"Would you like to take more time for yourself before going home?"

I nod. Definitely. Where is he going with this? Does he want to stay in Hawaii longer?

"Would you be interested in potentially flying back to my house to stay with me? You can stay for as long as you want."

Given our situation, I was not expecting that. I don't think people should know about us right now. I don't even know about us. Am I crazy if I say yes? I ended up doing this spontaneous thing, staying with him in Hawaii, so what's to lose…?

"That's sweet of you, but it's best if I stop hanging onto you and face my problems. I'm going to have to face them eventually." What would his friends and family think of me? That I'm some gold digger or something?

"It's no problem. I love your company. We had a pretty great time here. It's only been a week since all this happened. Giving yourself more time won't hurt anything."

It may not hurt anything, but I'm falling for him. What if I get hurt all over again? I sound crazy. I shouldn't even be in this situation…liking someone else while my cheating husband is at home. Why can't Jay just tell me how he feels? I don't want to be the one to bring things up.

"What would your friends and family think of all this?" I say.

"I don't care what they think. They don't have to know anything. I've been keeping to myself lately after everything that happened, and I've been busy. I would suggest we stay longer here, but I have some work I have to get back to."

"Are you saying I would be alone at your house?"

"No, I can do a lot from home. There are a lot of meetings that I have to attend. I love your company, and I'd really enjoy spending more time with you. I thought of this on a whim. Maybe it would help you, and I'd definitely enjoy you being around, too."

Jay gets back off the bed and starts folding more of his clothes. I continue watching him, contemplating my next move. Is it crazy for me to want to see where this goes? He's a nice guy. Even if we were to stay good friends, I would like his friendship. But then again, that would be hard with all the sexual attraction I feel for him. Friends with benefits could work. No. I can't do that. Jay isn't like that either.

"Before I say yes. Let me check with my boss and see if he's fine with me taking more time off," I say. I grab my phone and send a quick text over to him.

"I wonder if we'd even be able to change my flight." I say. Jay stays silent like he did something that he shouldn't have. "Jay?"

He looks up at me. "I already called this morning to see if it was something we could do before I suggested it."

"Oh." I get a ping on my phone. "My boss said it's fine. It's been slow, anyway." I look at Jay again. He looks like he needs to say something. I squint my eyebrows, confused. "What is it?"

"I'm glad you said yes, and I'm really happy your boss was fine with it because I already changed your flight this morning." His face looks like he's caught red-handed doing something bad.

This is the end of the road for him. It looks cute how scared he is.

"How did I not know this?"

"Are you mad? I saw your boarding pass sticking out of your suitcase while you were still asleep and called."

Laughing, I say, "No. I'm not mad. I guess I'm more surprised." Relief lifts from my shoulders. To be honest, I was not ready to face whatever I have to face when I get home. Jay is right. It has only been a week. More time is what I need. I was at least lucky enough to stay on vacation with someone. I'm sure many people who get cheated on don't get this kind of luxury. They have to face it right away.

"There is one more thing," Jay says.

I look up at him. Oh no, what did he do now? "You're full of surprises right now."

"I asked one of my friends to pick me up since he dropped me off at the airport. I didn't want my car sitting there for two weeks racking up a bill. We can call an Uber to pick us up."

That makes me a little nervous. But I guess they don't have to know everything. We could make up a better story.

"If you trust him, then I'm fine with it. Have you told him anything about us?"

"No, he doesn't have to know anything." Jay laughs. "We will keep him guessing. Eventually I'll say something. Not everything, though."

"I'm going to go update my mom, so she isn't worried." Déjà vu hits me as I walk out to the balcony to call my mom and tell her what my plans are now. I sat here a week ago to tell her I was going to stay here with a stranger. Lia keeps calling me too. I decide to update her.

> Me: Promise you won't freak out?

> Lia: Oh no! What are you doing now?

Me: I decided to go home with Jay and spend another week with him.

Lia: Where is my best friend? What have you done with her? I'm starting to think this isn't Lilah.

Lia: Why did I get sent to the principal's office in the third grade?

Me: What the hell Lia you have to be a little more specific?

Lia: I can't get too specific or I'll give the answer away.

Lia: Fine. I accidentally hit a girl with a what?

Me: Oh yeah! You threw a snowball at her that had a rock in it but you didn't know it had a rock in it. She cried in the principal's office and told them you threw a rock at her. There. Did I pass?

Lia: I guess! But I still don't understand what you're doing. I've already talked to your mom, and she thinks you're crazy. Does she know you're now going to his house?

Me: Yes, she does.

Lia: What made you decide this?

Me: I've been having a good time with him, and I really don't want to go home yet and face everything.

Lia: You can't run away forever

Me: I'm not. I'm giving myself more time.

Lia: Just be careful. I can't lose my best friend.

Me: I will. Nothing has happened to me so far.

Lia: That sounds reassuring

Lia: When you have time from your new love life can you call me and update me more?

Me: I promise. Muah!

It's official. My mom thinks I've lost it, and so does my best friend Lia. I guess I officially have.

CHAPTER TEN

As we walk out of the airport, I see Jay's hand go up as he waves down someone. A black pickup truck pulls up beside us. Jay's friend twists his face when he sees me. I've been questioning myself this past week, and now here I am going to spend another week with a stranger. At least he isn't as much of a stranger now.

I never would've imagined I'd do this, but I also never imagined Aiden would cheat on me either.

Jay's friend gets out and gives Jay a quick hug. He looks over at me, giving me a look as if I'm a lost puppy.

"Alex, this is Lilah. Lilah, this is Alex. He's one of my best friends." Alex reaches his hand out to me, and I extend my hand to shake his.

"Nice to meet you. I've heard great things about you," I say.

"Really? Because I have heard nothing about you." He gives Jay a little punch on the arm. Jay laughs.

We load our stuff in the truck and start driving to Jay's house. Jay insisted I sit in the front. The awkwardness sets in as I sit next to Alex, another stranger. No one breaks the silence as we drive through the busy streets. We go through the city until we hit a suburban area. I've never been here. It's pretty nice. Although I still haven't escaped the heat or humidity.

"So, is anyone going to talk?" Alex asks, staring straight ahead as he drives.

"What do you want to talk about?" Jays asks. The fact that he's questioning who I am, and Jay keeps acting as if nothing is happening, makes me laugh.

"I'm a stray that Jay found in Hawaii," I say.

"No, you're not. She's a friend Alex, and I wanted to show her around Texas since she has never been."

Alex looks at Jay through the rearview mirror. I'm trying to hold in my laughter while me and Jay play around with him. Alex's concerned voice makes me think he's wondering if Jay kidnapped me. This little game Jay and I have going on is making this situation a lot easier to handle.

"Jay, I have known you forever and I've never met this friend of yours before or heard of her," Alex says.

"I'm a long-lost friend," I blurt out. Jay has a smirk on his face as I look back at him. This is what we're going to do, play games, and I'm all for it.

We pull up to what I assume is Jay's house. Jay gets our bags and he and Alex carry them in. Shock overwhelms me when I see how empty his house is. Some boxes are here and there, but there's no decorations. It looks so bare in here. There are a few bar stools, a couch, and a TV mounted on the living room wall... but other than that, the place is pretty empty.

Jay looks over at me. "There isn't much here since I just moved in before the trip."

"I remember you telling me you just bought it, but I didn't know it was empty. Now I know why you asked me to come home with you; you want me to help unpack and decorate your place." I look over at Jay. "You're sneaky."

"What can I say? I don't have many women in my life. So, you're the one who lucked out with this job."

Alex looks between Jay and me. "Is anyone going to tell me what is going on?" We both stay silent. Alex walks over to the fridge and grabs himself a beer, pops it open, and chugs quite a bit before setting it down. As soon as he's finished, he looks at us again, clearly waiting for a real answer.

"Do you want something to drink?" Jay asks me.

"I'll have a beer," I say and look over at Alex who has made himself comfortable on the couch, still watching and waiting for an answer.

Jay hands me a beer as I take a seat on one of the bar stools. At least he has bar stools because there is no table, just a big empty space where the dining room is.

It's about six in the evening, and my stomach growls. "Are you hungry, Jay?"

"Yes. We could barbecue something."

"That sounds good. A home-cooked meal is what I need after all the eating out we have done." I take a large sip of my beer, still trying not to laugh at Alex while he continues to stare at us.

"Hello? Is anyone going to tell me what the hell is going on?" Jay and I both look over at him. "Oh good. You guys can see me. I'm not a ghost. I was starting to worry."

Jay gives me a questioning look if I'm okay with him telling him or not. "He won't say anything," he whispers.

I shrug my shoulders. "If you say so."

"We met in Hawaii. Lilah was going through a rough time, and she needed more time to get away, so I invited her back to my place," Jay explains.

He doesn't seem to question anything after that. He seems like a pretty easy-going guy. Maybe he won't care if he knows the truth. Jay doesn't seem to think he will.

"We met at a bar. I accidentally stole his seat and then everything took off from there." I smile at Alex, hoping that will calm his curiosity.

"What were you doing in Hawaii alone?" Alex asks me.

Jay interrupts. "She wasn't alone." He stops and his eyes go wide as if he said something wrong.

"What's wrong if she was alone or not?" Alex must see his face.

"Sorry. I didn't mean to blurt that out," Jay whispers to me.

I turn back to Alex, seeing confusion on his face. "I was there with a friend and things ended up going bad, and then I met Jay, so I spent the rest of the vacation with him."

"Okay," Alex says, apparently over with his brief interrogation. "Let's grill." He gets up from the couch and walks out to the back patio.

Well, that was easy. He's not so anal about his friend's new friend.

Since Jay doesn't have a table, we all sit down on the couch to eat. I start making a list in my mind of all the important everyday things he needs to get for his place. Considering all he's done for me, it's the least I can do for him.

"So, Alex, are you married or have a girlfriend?" I ask.

"Nah. Haven't found the right person." I wonder if he still lives with his parents then. He's old enough not to be.

"Do you live around here?" Jay chokes on his beer after asking that. Guilt arises from his face.

"I live next door." Well, that was something Jay forgot to mention. No wonder he's choking on his beer.

"Is that how you found this house?" I ask Jay, dipping a homemade fry in fry sauce and popping it into my mouth. When I started making my fry sauce, Jay and Alex looked at me weird. I explained to them it's a Utah thing. It's only mayo and ketchup mixed. I'm seriously surprised that more people don't do this.

"Yes, I lucked out. It went on the market just as I put my other house up for sale."

"You guys must be close if you two live right next door to each other," I say before carefully taking a bite of my hamburger.

Alex made these burgers so big it's hard to eat them and not look like a slob.

"We've known each other for a long time. He used to live with me when he emancipated—" He stops abruptly and looks over at Jay, then hurries and grabs his beer and chugs it.

"She knows."

So, this is the Alex, Jay talked about when he said his best friend took him in when he emancipated himself.

"I better get going. It's getting late." Alex stands up and takes his plate to the sink.

I sit up and face Alex in the kitchen. "It was nice to meet you. I'm sure I'll see you around."

"Oh, you will." Alex gives me a wink and walks out the front door.

After finishing my burger, I go into the kitchen to clean. Jay walks in as I rinse the dishes. "I'm sorry I didn't tell you he lived next door. Was that too much for you?"

The worry in his eyes makes me feel bad. I put him in this position, and he keeps second guessing what he should say.

"You have nothing to be sorry about. Your life is being interrupted by me. I really liked him. Your life can't stop because of me. He seems very easygoing." Putting the last of the dishes away in the dishwasher, I ask, "Where am I sleeping? A shower sounds nice, too."

"About that," he says.

"Oh, no. You're full of surprises."

"Since you know I barely moved in, I hardly have anything. I let Lindsee keep most of it because I wanted to start from scratch. I only have one bed right now and one shower that can be used because I only have one shower curtain. That's all in the master bedroom. The bedroom I use."

I walk over to Jay and pat his chest. "We have a lot of work to do here."

CHAPTER ELEVEN

AFTER WAKING UP BY SOMEONE THIS WEEK, IT FELT STRANGE waking up in an empty bed. Jay must be working. He said he had work he had to do.

Aiden crosses my mind while I try to wake up. For the past week, I have ignored both calls and text messages from him. Leaning over to the nightstand to grab my phone, I decide to listen to his latest voicemail. "Lilah. Where are you? I miss you. I've been staying away from the house, as you asked. I need to see you and talk to you. No one will tell me where you are. I understand why they won't. I don't deserve to know. I hope you're safe. I know we can work this out. You need to give me a chance." Irritation causes me to slam my phone down. His voicemail proves my point that he doesn't fully understand what he did or what I've been trying to get us to work on. It's all about him. It's been like this for a while. I this, I that. It's never a *we* or an *us*.

My heart sinks a little, not because I miss him, but because of how he asks me to give him another chance. He's delusional still. There is no way I can go back to that. To him. He ripped my heart out. No, he has been ripping my heart out little by little over the years. This was the final straw. There is no need to listen to all his voice mails. One by one, I go through and delete them all.

The last thing I want to do is disturb Jay while he works. Instead of looking for him, I head for the kitchen.

The coffee brews and the aroma fills up the kitchen as I prepare a cup for myself. The smell of coffee makes mornings so much better. Even though caffeine doesn't do much for me in the morning, the smell and taste wakes me up. After it's done brewing, I head outside to the backyard and take a seat on the cement stairs. There is a pond in the back of Jay's house, and the other house's backyards surround it, too, creating a circle.

I decided to finally give Lia a call. She's going to be so mad at me for ignoring her for this long. We tell each other everything, and I've been keeping her in the dark.

Lia picks up quickly. It only had to ring once. "Wow, I was starting to think I was chop liver to you now that you met some fancy guy on your fancy vacation." I knew she would have some smart-aleck remarks. That's why we get along so well. We are always straightforward with each other and not one of us gets mad about it.

We've been friends since our elementary school days. She knows everything about me, and I know everything about her. Both of us grew up without a father and neither of us had siblings. Our similarities connected us, and we've been inseparable since. The only difference between us is she never settled down young, and I did. I was worried it would change our friendship, but thankfully, nothing has come between us.

She's much more carefree that I am and decides on a whim without thinking of the consequences. She deals with those later. Growing up with a single parent had its benefits. She knew she never would depend on a man. Education was important to her, that way she knew she would have a good job to provide for herself if anything were to happen and she ended up alone. At times, her mom struggled to make ends meet after Lia's father walked out on them. Lia was only a toddler. Supposedly, it was too much for him to handle. Her parents were eighteen when they started dating, and never had a clue in the world what to do next after high school. What they didn't think would come next was a baby.

"I know. I've left you out of the loop. A lot has gone on in such a short amount of time. I would still rather tell you everything in person."

"Fine. I'm assuming you made it to his house?"

"Yes."

"How is it?"

I'm debating if I should tell her his house is empty. She's going to think he set me up since she doesn't know him. Lia is already iffy about this whole situation, even though she wants me to get out of my comfort zone. Believe me, this is way out of my comfort zone.

"It's a nice house. He just moved in, so there's a lot of unpacking and decorating to do. He also needs to get more furniture."

"So, you're going to play house with him?"

"No. But I will help him. He's been there for me when he didn't have to be. It's the least I can do." Hearing a noise coming from behind, I turn, and look over and see Jay standing by the sliding door.

He stops in his tracks. "Sorry, I didn't know you were on the phone," he says, whispering.

"It's okay. I'm going to get off." He shakes his head and walks back into the house. "Lia, can I call you later?"

"You know you won't call me later. You're too busy playing house," she says sarcastically.

"Love you too. I'll talk to you later."

When I walk back into the house, I find Jay in his office.

"Hey," I say.

"Good morning," he says. "Anything you want to do today?"

"It would be a good idea if we get you some furniture." I look around his office and note there isn't much in here, either. There's only a small desk and a chair. I immediately second guess my idea. What if we run into people he knows? I could say I'm his interior designer.

"Sounds like a plan." He gives me a wink. "I'll finish some work while you get ready."

The clothes I brought were enough to last a week. I'm having a hard time finding something to wear. Everything has already been used. At least I brought enough bras and underwear. I usually always bring extras just in case. *Just in case what? I pee my pants?* I think to myself. Who knows, but I guess it's a good thing I did. Never know when you're going to meet a stranger on vacation and *play house* with him. Always expect the unexpected.

I feel like we're going through a maze as we zig zag through the furniture store. It has everything anyone could possibly need for a house. Jay wasn't too sure what to get. On the way over here, I was showing him some ideas on Pinterest. "What do you want to look at first?" I ask.

"Let's go with the big items to get those out of the way. I can take my time with decorating." He grabs my hand and leads me to the dining room tables. I'm hesitant at first to reciprocate hand holding. We've never held hands before. I figured he'd be worried in case we run into someone, but I'm assuming he doesn't care.

Jay finds a washed-out dining room table pretty quickly. I told him it would be easier to decorate around neutral colors. His couch is already a light gray color. Jay grabs my hand again and we head over to the couches to find a coffee table. I'm surprised at how comfortable I am holding his hand out in public.

As we are walking over to the couches we both take a seat on one of them and put our feet up on one of the coffee tables in front of us. Jay rests his head on my shoulder. I bring my hand up and run my fingers through his hair. A soft yawn comes from him.

"Are you tired?"

I feel Jay's head nod. I look down at him and his eyes are kind of closed.

"What time did you wake up?"

"Five o'clock."

"Why did you wake up so early?"

"I've been off work for two weeks. I have a lot to catch up on."

"That's going to be me next week."

Jay squeezes my knee and raises his head from my shoulder. "Let's keep looking or I'm going to fall asleep."

We both get up and start looking around all the coffee tables they have in between the couches. I spot a light brown one and point over to it.

"This one looks like it would match with your couch."

"Okay, I trust you, let's get it," he says.

"You've been agreeing with everything I pick out. You don't have to."

I sit down on one of the couches facing the coffee table making sure it will look good. Jay comes and sits next to me and says, "I really do like it. Have you done this before? You're really good at it."

"I have a few times. Haven't you? Since you've had your own place before and I'm assuming you lived with Lindsee?"

"When I first moved out on my own I was too poor to afford anything. I mostly got hand me downs. When me and Lindsee moved in together she bought everything."

"She bought everything without you? She didn't even check to see if you liked it first?"

"Pretty much," he says and gets up from the couch. He reaches for my hand and lifts me up from the couch. "Let's go look at their patio sets."

We start walking over to the patio furniture, and I hear someone yell Jay's name. An older couple starts walking over to us, and Jay suddenly stops when he registers his name being called. His body jerks back as if he got shocked. By the looks of him, he looks stunned to see them. Who is this couple that is making him act like this? He hasn't let go of me, which tells me maybe it doesn't bother him to be seen holding my hand.

"Hi, how are you guys?" Jay asks the couple as they approach us. They are now both standing in front of us with confused looks on their faces. I debate whether or not I should introduce myself or not.

"Hi," I say.

"We're good," the older lady says to Jay before turning toward me. "Hello. I'm Karen and this is my husband, Mike." She reaches out and shakes my hand.

"This is Lilah," Jays says.

"Hi, nice to meet you."

"Jay, could we talk to you in private?" Karen says.

My eyes are roaming between all three of them, confused by what is going on.

"Whatever you have to say, you can say in front of Lilah." Silence rolls through her, like she's never been told no before.

"Honey let's leave them alone," Mike says, grabbing his wife's hand and trying to get her to leave. She rips her hand out of his, staring at us.

"Jay, Lindsee misses you very much. There is still a chance for you two if you forgive her and move on from it all. I know she created a mess, but everyone deserves a second chance. You two were so good together." She looks at me and smiles. A smile that is more of a no-offense smile.

My face falls. I'm dumbfounded by these people. Do they

even know what she did? Jay looks as dumbfounded as me when I see his face. Mike standing there, shaking his head, embarrassed by his wife.

"Karen, Mike, with all due respect, your daughter is a whore. You can't turn a whore into a housewife. I'm looking for someone I can settle down with one day and start a family of my own with. It would be a shame for me to stoop that low and give her a second chance. Some people don't deserve second chances, and your daughter is one of them."

Daughter? What the fuck. These are Lindsee's parents.

A loud gasp comes from Karen, like that's the worst thing she has ever heard. But Damn Jay sure told her. That response even surprised me.

"Lilah and I have more shopping to do. Have a great day." Jay leads me away, his hand in mine, as we both smile.

We're beat by the time we're done shopping. On the way home, we grabbed some Chinese food. We were too tired to go to a restaurant so we're both settled on the floor to eat and watch a movie.

"Hey, sorry about Lindsee's parents earlier today," Jay says.

"There is nothing for you to be sorry about. I'm sure running into them wasn't planned." I take a bite of my shrimp fried rice. It tastes so good. I don't remember the last time I had Chinese food.

"I'm sure it was still awkward for you. I never expected her to ask me to get back with Lindsee."

"It shocked me when she said that," I say with my mouth full of food. Jay hasn't touched his food yet, and I'm over here eating like a pig.

"I never liked her mom. She was always in our business, always deciding for us. Lindsee would go along with it."

"Her name suits her then," I say and we both start laughing.

I couldn't imagine Aiden's parents coming up to me and asking me to give Aiden a second chance. Jay handled it, though. I would have exploded on them. It hurts to know Jay grew up with no family at all. Being bounced around from house to house. Never having a steady family. The way he talks about his life, it sounds like he has always been content with it, always putting one step in front of the other.

CHAPTER TWELVE

I'M WAITING IN THE KITCHEN WHILE JAY WALKS IN WITH GROCERY bags around both arms. He wouldn't let me grab any, and he insisted on doing it in one trip. He sets them down on the counter, and we both start pulling food out of the bags and putting it away. I get this déjà vu feeling. Weird, I can't place where it's coming from. I think more on it and realize maybe it's because the two of us are putting groceries away, moving seamlessly around his kitchen like an old married couple.

This feels like when Aiden and I would go grocery shopping together. We used to always go together in the evening in the middle of the week because it was less busy at that time. We would come home and put the food away together, always leaving out what we were going to eat for dinner that night. After the groceries were away, we would work on dinner together.

I can't believe I forgot about this. It was one thing we always enjoyed doing together. I always appreciated him for helping me because I know a lot of men leave it up to the woman to do that. As if it's the woman's job. I would always thank him after. He would tell me not to thank him because a marriage is fifty-fifty.

It makes me wonder when that stopped—and why it stopped.

It's one of those little things that made such an impact, and I didn't realize how much of an impact it made until he stopped. It's those types of actions that make a marriage work. No one knows how significant little things can impact a marriage until they go through it. It makes me sad to think Aiden and I got to this point without even realizing it.

Did I stop grocery shopping or did he? I can't even remember. I used to enjoy doing that with him, and now I can't even remember why it stopped, let alone that it even happened. I feel the urge to text him and ask him if he remembers. It can't only be me that forgets these memories. This shouldn't have ever been a memory left in the back of my head to be stored away. It shouldn't have ever stopped to turn into a memory.

I grab my phone and have almost a hundred messages from him I've been ignoring. I put his messages on silent. It stops notifying me when his texts come through. I can see he has texted by the number of text messages rising. I decide against texting him and put my phone down out of reach.

Jay fills a pot with water for the spaghetti we are going to make. I grab a frying pan and start on the meat sauce. I can't help but keep thinking about Aiden. The déjà vu feels so real right now, and I don't know how to stop it from consuming me.

I continue frying the meat, trying to shake this feeling off. Jay has now turned on some music while we work in tandem in the kitchen. I glance over at him, watching him put the last of the groceries away. He sees me glancing at him and walks over to me, then wraps his arms around me and kisses my neck. A tingling sensation runs down my body.

"What are you thinking about?" he asks.

"Nothing, just admiring you."

"What's there to admire?"

"You being you."

He bends down and kisses my neck again. I give him a slight smile and turn back to the stove. Not a lot of words are being spoken, just actions that I have been needing. Actions that I've wanted and needed from Aiden for so long.

My chest constricts, thinking about all the times I waited and waited for these actions from Aiden and I never received them. It always made me feel like I wasn't worth his time. Like I was one of those ex-wives where the husband doesn't put in effort but puts in effort with his new wife. The effort that the ex-wife was needing. Those situations have always crushed me when I see them. Why wasn't his first wife good enough for him to save the marriage? The second wife comes along, and he makes all the effort in the world. I've seen it happen once to a friend of mine. Never understood why she wasn't good enough. I could tell it hurt her a little, seeing what she needed from her ex-husband play out in front of her with someone else. She never let us believe she was hurting from it. Sometimes people make little sense. I guess it's better to stop it than to force it to happen. But when should you realize enough is enough?

CHAPTER THIRTEEN

TEXAS HEAT IS NO JOKE IN AUGUST. THE HUMIDITY IS A LITTLE rough, too. My state is so dry. I'm not used to this. Jay has a good client of his that lets him use his country club for free. He's done a lot of contracting work for him, and always ensures he gets the best subcontractors to do the jobs that he needs done for his club. He appreciates how hard he works for him, so in return, he gets in for free.

We're both sitting out by the pool. Jay feels bad when he works because I'm left with nothing to do or left home alone. He has computer work to do today, so he took me here so I wouldn't be at home bored while he works. They have an open bar for members. Jay technically isn't a paying member, but I've been using this open bar to my advantage. Every time the waiter comes with my drink, we tip them.

I'm not sure how much it costs to be a member. If they have an open bar for members, I couldn't imagine the monthly price. Especially with everything else they have here. There's a golf course that wraps around the entire club, two fancy restaurants with bars inside, tennis, pickleball, and basketball courts, an open gym, a pool with an outside bar and small cafe.

I felt out of place when we arrived. It's a lot of older people that look bougie and settled more in life. I look around, wondering what everyone does for a living to afford this. Jay made a comment that he would never pay for this. He hardly ever comes. He said he never cared to bring Lindsee here. The money got to her head, and she wanted to spend it on extravagant purchases.

I'm four drinks in and I'm getting drunk. I lean over to look at Jay's computer. "What are you doing?" I ask flirtatiously.

"Working." He gives me the side-eye.

"Do you want to join in on the free drinks?" He looks over at me and squints his eyebrows.

"Is someone getting drunk with these free drinks?" I slowly take a sip of my drink from my straw and look up at him. My lips raise a little, giving him a small little smirk.

The next thing I know, Jay slams his computer shut, grabs our bags over his shoulder, and stands up fast. So fast I'm looking at him, confused. He reaches out for my hand, and I give it to him. He leads us out of the club before I can even ask what's happening.

He throws the bags in the back of the truck. I stand still, just watching him. What the hell did I do?

"Did I do something wrong?" I ask once we're driving. I'm so confused at this point. He doesn't look mad. Maybe I'm reading this all wrong. I am pretty drunk. His expression is blank when I look over at him. He looks at me and then back down to his swim trunks. My eyes trail to where his are focused and I see a bulge in his swim trunks.

I laugh. "I'm glad I have that effect on you." His cheeks redden as he remains silent. "Would you like me to take care of it?"

I hear a grunt from him. "Not unless you want me to crash." He's fixing his shorts and moving them down a little, rearranging his bulge. We're both quiet the entire way home. I keep peeking over and Jay still has his bulge popping out. It's making me wet looking at it, knowing I did that to him.

We pull up to the house and Jay shifts the vehicle into park. "Get in the house," he says with a raspy voice.

"Hmmm." This silent banter and bossiness is something I have never seen. It turned me on more than I ever thought. I move fast through the garage door and pass the mudroom. I get myself into the kitchen when I'm suddenly being picked up and placed on the counter next to the fridge. Jay grabs my face and crashes his lips onto mine. We press our lips together, feeling the heat from one another's breath. Running my hands up and down his torso, I feel his body heat. I grab his shirt and pull it up over his head. He spreads my legs wider and gets in between, feeling our bodies pressed together. The counter and his height are the right size for both of us. He moves his hips in a circular motion around my center, and a rush surges through me as I feel his cock pulsing on my vagina. I run my hands down his torso a little lower to feel his cock.

"I was wondering when you guys were going to be back home. I've been so bo—" All three of us freeze in place. Jay and I were so into each other we forgot to close the garage door. We didn't hear Alex walk through it.

"Alex, what are you doing?" Jay groans. His head falls and rests on my shoulder. His breathing is shallow. I can't tell if he's breathing hard from us or if he's pissed Alex walked in.

"What are you doing? It looks like you're humping the counter." The fridge is blocking me from the view Alex is standing at. I look over at him and smile.

Alex gasps. "Oh shit." Jay backs away and I jump off the counter.

"Hi, Alex. You came at the perfect time. I was about to whip Jay's cock out." I look down at Jay's cock and the bulge is gone. Looking back up at him in disappointment.

"You're such a bastard," Jay says to Alex. Jay picks up his shirt from the ground and throws it on.

"The garage door was open. Why didn't you lock it?" Alex asks.

"Fuck off."

Alex slaps Jay on the back like a brotherly thing to do at a time like this. I can't help but laugh. "See, she's not mad."

"Oh no, I'm mad, but I'm drunk and hungry. You're buying us dinner. I'll be in the shower. Please have dinner here by the time I'm done." I walk between both of them, gliding my hand over Jay's chest, and walk upstairs.

CHAPTER FOURTEEN

I feel bad about how things ended last night between Jay and me. It wasn't our fault, but still. Alex is so clueless. It was hard to be mad at him because of how oblivious he was. A normal person would run out the door if they saw that. Instead, he thought Jay was humping the counter. I can't help but laugh every time I think about it. The fridge couldn't have blocked me that much, plus my feet were hanging off the counter. He should have seen my legs by Jay's. Oh well. I can't blame the guy, that's apparently just who Alex is.

I want to do something for Jay. He's been there for me so much and keeping my mind occupied so I don't have to think about the uninvited. I remember him telling me about a job site he has to be at. He said he would be out of the house all day. I walk over to his office to see if there is an address written somewhere. There isn't one. With my luck, it's on his computer.

After about ten minutes, I'm at a loss. There's nothing. I sit in his office chair thinking about what he told me about it. He told me that the building was being turned into something else. I can't remember what he told me it was. He said it was about ten minutes from his house, and that if I needed anything he could be home fast. I pull out my phone and Google places. There is a movie theater that has been closed for a while. Maybe that is it. I can't find anything else that isn't up and running. This must be it.

Half an hour later my Uber is outside waiting for me. "Could you take me to Chick-fil-A?" I ask.

"Of course," he says.

Ten minutes later we pulled up into Chick-fil-A. I'm scanning the menu but not sure what Jay likes or if he even likes this place.

"What do you get when you eat here?" I ask the driver.

"I always order the number one. I never adventure out too much when it comes to food," he says and shrugs his shoulders.

"Can I get the number one with a coca cola and a southwest salad?" I ask over the intercom. "Do you want anything?" I ask the driver.

He shakes his head no.

"That's all. Thank you."

We pull out of the Chick-fil-A drive-through and he asks, "Do you have the address you want me to drop you off at?"

I pull my phone out and show him the address on google maps. He plugs it into his GPS. "Are you sure you want to go there? That place has been closed for about ten years."

"Yes. I heard it's being rebuilt into something."

Many people are working in the old building. This must be the place. I look around for Jay's truck in case it's not. When I spot it, I say to the driver, "It's here. Thanks for the ride."

I exit the car and walk to the building. It's gutted down to nothing. The roof is standing up by columns. I walk inside and look around for Jay. A lot of the workers are looking at me. I get a feeling I shouldn't be here. No one talks to me or says anything.

I spot Jay and walk toward him. His back is to me. Someone is standing in front of him talking. I get a little closer.

The guy Jay is talking to spots me and looks back at Jay. He tilts his head toward me. He doesn't look very happy, and suddenly I'm worrying I made a huge mistake. Jay turns around and his eyes are on me with his eyebrows raised and then the next they're squinting with his jaw tight and hard. Jay turns his head back to the man he was talking to before and then turns back to me. I look over at the guy and he's walking away, shaking his head.

"What are you doing here?" Jay states, sounding angry.

I lift the Chick-fil-A bag. "I wanted to bring you lunch?" Jay grabs my hand and walks me out of the building quickly. I'm trying to keep up with his speed, but my legs aren't as long as his. I pull my hand out of his and stop. "Do not pull me like that." Jay tries to grab my hand again and I pull away.

"Lilah, you're not supposed to be in here. It's dangerous and you don't even have a hard hat on." He tries again to grab my hand, but I keep it down to my side and walk away from him. He is following me out now. Once I'm out of the building, I keep walking. "Lilah, stop!" Jay yells.

"What?" I pause and turn my head over my shoulder.

"You can't just show up at my job like this. It's dangerous and you don't have the proper safety gear on. If something were to happen with you in there I would have been in a lot of shit." Jay says. Wide eyed at how angry he is. I stand there in silence. Jay reaches into his pocket and hands me his keys. "Go home. I'll find a ride." He turns around and walks back into the building.

I watch him walk away with his back toward me. He walks in urgency with his shoulder up right. His fists are down by his side. His hands are clenched into fists so tightly his veins are popping out of his arms. He looks like he's about to knock someone out. The other men move out of his way when he walks back into the building. Once he passes them, they look back at him and then at me, just as confused as I am. I stood there watching him walk away from me in shock and disbelief that he got this upset. What the fuck just happened?

I'm in the middle of watching *The Proposal* when I hear a knock on the door. The time on my phone is almost seven. Getting up from the couch, I see Jay through the window. I open the door and move to the side for him to pass me. He walks in and reaches his hand out to mine. I place my hand in his and he walks us to the couch. This isn't the reaction I was expecting. I thought he would come home mad.

"I'm sorry for the way I acted. That job has been stressful. The job is behind because a lot of our sub-contractors haven't shown up. The owner is upset because of how behind it is. He came in to see for himself what had been going on. When it gets to the point where the owner has to come in and check out what is going on, I know all trust is gone, and that's not a good thing." He stops and looks at me before grabbing my hand and placing a kiss on it. "I shouldn't have pulled you out like that. I'm embarrassed by my actions. The owner was already mad and when he saw you walking in with no safety equipment, that upset him even more. It shows how I've been running this job, and it wasn't a good look on me."

I sit here in silence. Not sure what to say. No one has ever apologized to me with an explanation. I only get one word. And that's always a sorry. I squeeze Jay's hand and say, "I was trying to do something nice for you after everything you've been doing for me. I should have asked if it was okay to come by. I hope I didn't get you into more trouble?"

"Nothing I couldn't handle." He leans back into the couch. "I'm up for eating the food you picked up for me. Where is it?" Jay looks around.

"I tossed it."

"Why?"

"Because at that point, I didn't think you deserved it."

"You're right. I didn't." Jay leans back into the couch and pulls me to him. He puts his arm around me. I snuggle up closer to him and lay my head against his chest before reaching for the remote to turn the movie back on.

CHAPTER FIFTEEN

THERE IS A NOTE, AND A RED ROSE ON JAY'S PILLOW. I GRAB THE rose and smell it. I wonder where he got this from. We didn't get flowers last night. My attention is drawn to the note as I read it.

I'll be in and out of meetings all day today. I forgot to mention it to you last night. Call me if you need anything. I'll try to get back as soon as I can.

This is a nice way to wake up. I stay in bed for a little longer, enjoying the relaxing time I have left. It's been nice having this break from work. Especially after what happened. After the first night in Hawaii, I didn't think meeting Jay would happen either. I keep trying not to think too much about it because I know when I get home, my world is going to come crashing down.

I swing my legs over off the bed and walk to my suitcase that

I have in the corner. Jay is also waiting on a dresser to be delivered. For now, his clothes are hanging in the closet with his socks and underwear in plastic bins. I throw on some leggings and a tank top and head downstairs to get some coffee. The second I get off the last step of the stairs, I see another note folder in half sitting upright on the kitchen island. I walk over and read it.

Look in the microwave.

I walk over to the microwave, then pull the door open. I see waffles on a plate with another note.

Look in the fridge.

I open the fridge and there is a bowl of fruit and a side of Nutella with yet another note.

Enjoy the fruit and Nutella with your waffles. -
Jay

My cheek heat as I smile from ear to ear. I don't remember the last time I had something like this done for me. Aiden used to do cute stuff like this, but it's been ages. Too long for me to even remember. I get sick butterflies in my stomach thinking about him. I hurry, erase him out of my mind and start preparing my waffles to eat. The time will come soon when my focus is on him again. The uninvited. Eventually, I will have to face everything.

After I'm done eating, I'm trying to figure out what to do for the day. I don't have a car to go anywhere. Debating what I should do for Jay, I look around the kitchen and see some boxes with the word *kitchen* scribbled on it. I grab some scissors and start cutting open the boxes. This must be where all his dishes are. He only has a few here and there. I throw my hair in a bun, turn on Spotify, and start unpacking.

A few hours later, I'm taking the last empty box to the garage. Wiping the sweat from my forehead, I looked at the time and realized most of the day has gone by. That was quick. Jay should be home from work in a few hours. I decide a shower is much needed after all the sweating I've done.

Once I get out of the shower, I spot a robe. Wondering whose it is, I reach over and smell it. It has no scent, not even Jay's. I hope it's not Lindsee's. No. It shouldn't be. He said he moved here without her, and none of her stuff came to this house. I don't think it's another girl. He said he hasn't had time to date since the fallout from his almost marriage. Maybe he's just a man that likes robes. I shrug my shoulders and throw the robe on anyway.

Unpacking has left me more tired than I expected. Reaching for the TV remote, I scroll for a movie. Netflix needs to work on their movie selections. It's always the same shit. I decide on *How to Lose a Guy in 10 Days.*

The next thing I know, I wake up to Jay sitting on the couch next to me. I look down at myself to see if I'm covered. I fell asleep with only the robe on. He looks over at me and chuckles.

"How long have you been sitting there?" I ask while I sit up.

"About an hour."

"An hour?" I laugh. I look at my phone, and it says it's almost seven in the evening. That means I slept for a few hours. I wonder what he thought of me being naked under here. The other day we were so close to having sex, or at least I think that's where things were headed. We're always so close, but then something happens. I decide to give him a tease.

"Have you had dinner?" I say while moving the robe off my legs so close that any other movement would expose me. The robe's opening is shaped like a V, exposing the sides of my breasts a little. Jay looks over and stares down at my legs.

He clears his voice and says, "No." Even with his one-word answer, I can hear a slight shake to his voice.

I cross my legs up on the couch and slouch a little more down, not quite exposing myself, but enough for me to feel the air circulate around my center. I'm getting warm thinking about him grabbing me.

His eyes are gazing at me. I know I'm making him nervous.

"What do you want to eat?" I ask as I get on all fours and crawl over to him. My face is so close to his I see his chest rising with shallow breaths. I touch my lips to his, just enough to give him a tease. The robe isn't covering my breast so much anymore. I see him looking down at them and back up at me. He needs to touch me. I already feel myself getting wet for him. I go down to his neck and kiss him while blowing a little bit of air. Goosebumps rise on his skin. This better be enough of a tease.

"I'll go get dressed so we can go eat," I say as I'm stand and walk away from him. He grabs me by the waist and pulls me onto his lap. His lips immediately land on my neck, and the robe falls, exposing me more. His hand runs down my legs and back up to my midsection, along the sides of my breast and back down. I feel him harden beneath me as he rubs himself on my ass. I turn my head and kiss him. My body responds so well to him. I grab both of his hands and put one on my vagina and the other on my breast. He grabs my nipple and twists it between two of his fingers. His other hand teases all around my center. Our breathing becomes heavier and heavier as he makes circle motions on my clit. His cock pulsates beneath me, his circular motion becomes faster. My entire body tenses as heat rises through my body. I turn away from him and arch my back, my head resting on his shoulder. I shake as an orgasm releases through me, my heavy breathing transforming into moans.

I relax once the release is gone. Jay lays me on my back and takes off his shirt. He positions himself between my legs and starts kissing my stomach to my lips. I run my hands down his chest to his pants and release him. I grab him and run my hands up and down his shaft. He's dripping wet with pre-cum. I grab some of it and rub it around his head, making him moan a little. I lift my legs higher, and I make circular motions with his tip to the entrance of my vagina.

"Are you sure about this?" he asks, pausing.

"I'm so sure," I say, panting.

As I release my hands, he moves a little more inside. My back arches as he enters me. I feel the heat between our bodies continue to rise as he speeds up the rhythm, his own body tensing. He pulls out and jacks himself off, and I reach down and grab his balls just as he explodes everywhere. He lays his head on my shoulder while catching his breath.

It's in this moment that I feel an even deeper connection to him, like our bodies were made to be together.

"I wasn't expecting that." He gets up and walks toward the bathroom, and moments later, he walks back over to me with a washcloth.

"Is that a good or bad thing?" I ask.

He lowers himself to my lips and kisses me, whispering, "It's a very good thing."

CHAPTER SIXTEEN

AFTER GOING TO THE TARGET, I PULL UP TO JAY'S DRIVEWAY. I wanted to get some clothes. For the past week and a half, I've been washing the same clothes. There is another car outside. I wonder who is here. Jay stayed home to get some work done while I left.

As I grab the bags out of the truck, I can see a woman through the window. She looks familiar but I can't pinpoint why. It can't be someone I know. I try to open the front door, but it's locked. Weird. I set my bags down and I ring the doorbell. The woman opens the door. My eyes go wide. What the fuck is going on?

"Hi, can I help you?" she asks.

"Where is Jay?" I ask with a bite to my tone. Why is this bitch here? Have they set me up? Jay wouldn't do that. So many thoughts run through my mind. I push past her and go inside. I yell Jay's name and hear him run down the stairs.

"Why the fuck is this bitch here?" I yell. He looks at me, confused.

"I needed to give some paperwork to her. This is Lindsee." My mouth drops.

"*This* is Lindsee?" I say as I point to her.

"Who is this, Jay?" Lindsee asks with her hands on her hips.

I look over at her. "Do you not recognize me?"

"Should I?"

"Given what you did, you definitely should." I drop my bags on the floor and move a little closer to her. She flinches a little.

"What's going on?" Jays asks

I stare straight into her eyes. "Would you like to tell him or should I?"

She shrugs her shoulders, playing dumb. Lindsee walks over closer to Jay. "I don't know who you are or why you are here. We were having a nice evening together, and you rudely interrupted us."

"Oh, did I?" I ask sarcastically as I look over at Jay. "Was I being set up this whole time?" My mind is going in circles. How could this be? This can't be a coincidence. The room is spinning. I can't keep up with all this bullshit that keeps happening.

Jay moves closer to me. Reaching for my hand. I don't reciprocate. "Lilah, I really don't know what you are talking about. How would I have set you up?" Jay asks.

"This is the bitch that Aiden slept with when we were in Hawaii." I point toward her.

"What? It was Lindsee?" Jay looks over at Lindsee. "Is this true?"

"Ugh. Why does it matter? We weren't together, and he said he was single."

I knew she knew who I was. What does she mean by they *weren't* together? Did she come over here to get back with Jay? Are they talking about getting back together? I thought she was in the wrong place, but maybe it's me in the wrong place. My chest tightens. Tears threaten, the familiar feeling stinging my eyes, but I hold them in. I don't want to cry in front of this bimbo.

"What is she talking about, Jay? Are you guys getting back together?"

"Yes," Lindsee quickly says.

I look over at both of them, and she is trying to grab his hand.

He pulls his hand away from her and says, "What? No. She came over to get some papers that got mixed up with mine during the move." Jay lifts the papers up to show me. "I didn't know if any drama would start if she came and you were here, so I had her come when you were out."

That makes it sound like he was trying to hide something. Not knowing what to believe and trusting Jay so fast makes it harder to think. I trusted one man for so long and got screwed over by him. I should've kept my guard up and saved myself from all this trouble. Why did I put myself in this situation?

"What were you doing in Hawaii, Lindsee?" Jay turns to her.

"Jay, I love you. I want you back. My life hasn't been the same. I can't eat or sleep. I've been so depressed and—"

"That doesn't answer my question," he says, cutting her off.

"What do you think I was doing? I was trying to get you back." she says.

"You're a homewrecker, Lindsee. You ruined Noah's family, ours, and now Lilah's. I don't want you back after everything you've done," Jay says.

"But I learned my lesson after Noah. I regret what I did." Lindsee walks closer to Jay.

It's all three of us in this little circle in front of the front door. I debate if I should walk out or not, and they can sort all this out. I back away a little.

"You didn't learn your lesson because now you wrecked another family. Hers." Jay points to me.

"Who is she to you, anyway? If I slept with her so-called husband, why is she here?"

"That is none of your business," Jay says.

She is right. What am I doing here? I can't do this. This reminds me of some rom-com movie. I can't be in the middle of this. If they were done like Jay said they were, she wouldn't be here like this. There is no room for me to talk. I'm still married. My own life is messed up. Realizing that I cannot defend myself in this situation, I head upstairs.

"Where are you going?" Jay asks.

I ignore him and keep walking. I hear Jay tell Lindsee that they are through, and it will never work. Once I get to the room, I lock the door. Tears stream down my cheeks as I finally allow myself to cry, somehow feeling even more lost than I did when I walked in on Aiden. That woman is such a homewrecker. I grab my phone and find an Uber to come get me. It says it will take forty minutes. That should give me enough time to pack.

I grab my suitcase and throw it on the bed just as a knock sounds from the door. I stay quiet.

"Lilah, please open the door," Jay pleads. "Can we talk? Please?"

I wipe my tears from my face and open the door to let him in. After all, it's his house. Not letting him into his own room doesn't feel right.

Jay walks in and freezes. "Why are you packing?"

"I don't belong here, Jay. I should have never come. It's obvious you have unfinished business and so do I. This situation isn't something I should have kept going."

Jay grabs my hands and pulls me to him. He wipes my tears. "I knew the situation you were in. It's not all on you."

I turn away from him and continue folding my clothes.

He grabs my hands softly. "Stop. You're not leaving."

I pull my hands away from him, not wanting to look at him. "It's best if I go. I was leaving in a few days, anyway."

"I still want to spend those few days with you here. I don't want you to leave."

I fix my eyes on him as I say, "Are you hiding something from me? Why would you care if Lindsee saw me here or not?"

"Don't do this."

"Do what? You know what, I'm not even in the right situation myself to be asking that question. I was blinded and got cheated on. I'm stupid for falling for you, and I would be stupid if I stayed," I say.

"Lilah don't go. She means nothing to me. There is no way I would get back with her after what she did to me and now you."

Tears stream down my face again. "I can't do this. Someone has already hurt me. I need time for myself, and you deserve to find someone who's not in the mess I'm in."

"What does that mean?"

"I'm still married, Jay. You don't deserve that." A notification comes through my phone letting me know my Uber is here.

Jay stops me from opening the front door. He looks me in the eye. "Please don't do this. Don't leave on bad terms."

"Jay let her go if she doesn't want to stay," Lindsee says.

I'm surprised she's still here. I thought she left. Jay is too nice to throw her out. I'm sure he would never do that, and she knows it, so she's taking advantage of getting him to talk to her.

"I'm not leaving on bad terms. You deserve better, and I need to figure out my shit. You need to figure this situation out, too."

"That's bullshit."

I want him to. This past week and a half has been so good. He made me feel more than I've ever felt with someone. I have to let him go. He deserves more, and I need time.

I step up on my toes and kiss Jay on the lips. "It's not our time yet." As I get into the car, I look up at the porch where Jay is still standing. The driver drives away, and I realize this might be the last time I will ever see him. I turn my head and look away before the distance makes him disappear.

CHAPTER SEVENTEEN

As I'm waiting to board the plane, I text my mom and let her know when I'll be landing and ask if she can pick me up. I pull out the book I picked up at Target and try to get some reading in. Ten minutes later I look up and can't even remember what I've read. There is too much on my mind, and even the book can't distract me.

My whole body trembles as mountains come into view. The closer we get to landing, the more jittery I become. I can't avoid this situation forever.

My mom is waving me down as I walk outside the airport. I walk over and she gives me a hug. She grabs my suitcase from me and puts it in her back seat. We haven't said a word to each other yet. I'm too exhausted to talk. What do I even say? I made a fool out of myself.

She looks over at me. "Are you going to tell me where you have been?"

I sigh. "It's a long story. I don't have the energy to talk about it."

"You look sad and hurt. Nothing bad happened. Did it?"

"No." *Unless you're talking about Aiden cheating on me and finding out the guy I met and started falling for was engaged to the whore Aiden slept with.* No, I'm not hurt. I don't even know what to feel right now.

"Do you want to talk about Aiden and what you are going to do?"

"I'm divorcing him, Mom." I stare out the window, watching cars drive past us. She's driving slower than usual, to get more out of me before we get to my house.

My mom and I have always been so close. Growing up without a father, I guess it is bound to happen. I never knew exactly what happened with her and my father. I never cared. She filled that void for me, and I honestly didn't even notice he was missing. She dated here and there. Nothing serious. It was a blessing that she and my father never worked out. She's so content being alone, dating and having all her free time whenever she wants. At this point in her life, I can't see her letting a man have any say in her life.

"I know you are. I mean, are you staying at the house, or is he?"

"I told him to move out once I got home. Since the day I picked up my stuff from the hotel, I haven't spoken to him. He better have left."

"He doesn't know about the other week you spent with this mysterious friend of yours?"

"No. You're the only one that knows. Well, Lia, but I trust her not to say anything." I lean back into the seat and rest my head, staring out into the open road ahead of us. Looking out into the darkness that has already consumed me.

"Are you ever going to tell me about this friend?"

I sigh and tell her everything from the day Aiden and I landed in Hawaii, Jay and I in Hawaii and the week I spent at his house. Maybe it's best I get this off my chest. I finish telling her everything, and she stays silent. Is my mom disappointed in me? Is she shocked? She's not saying anything. "Are you going to say anything?" I ask.

"I guess I'm surprised."

"What surprised you the most?" My mom stays silent.

"Mom?"

"I'm trying to process it all. Even though you and Aiden had problems, I am surprised by it all. But I never expected him to do that. And then you spent almost two weeks with some guy you just met."

"It was only a week and a half."

"It hurts me you were hurting after what Aiden did. I'm your mom. When you are heartbroken, so am I. But I'm not even sure if you were heartbroken over Aiden. You sound more heartbroken over Jay."

I never stopped and thought of it that way. Am I more heartbroken over Jay? Sometimes I wanted Aiden to do something to push me over the edge to end our marriage. I thought that would be easier than going through with repairing it. I loved him too much to end it myself. But really…did I truly love him? Was I comfortable with him enough to stay and try to fix it? I felt more pain walking away from Jay than I did when I walked away from Aiden. I thought that was because of everything I had been through the past couple of weeks and the pain finally caught up with me—but maybe I'm wrong.

When you've been with someone for so long, it's hard to tell what to feel. It's hard to know what to do. I thought I was still in love with Aiden because I was so used to what we had. I was so used to *him*. I didn't stop and think about myself and what I wanted.

What I *needed*.

I look over at my mom. "Do you think I was over Aiden before I even realized it?"

"Love and relationships are complicated. If you felt like you needed to work on your marriage, I believe that was what you thought was best for you. Along the way, you probably fell out of love with Aiden and you were trying to get it back. You might not have known you fell out of love with him because no one wants to believe they fell out of love with their spouse. It's hard to come to terms with. People avoid it because it's easier than acknowledging it."

We pull up to my driveway, and I'm feeling a little relieved that no lights are on in the house. There are real-life problems I need to handle right now. I can't play hooky forever. I get out of the car and grab my suitcase. My mom comes around and asks, "Do you want me to go in with you?"

"No, I'll be fine. I'm exhausted and want to go to bed," I say.

"Let me know if you need anything. I love you." My mom leans in and gives me a hug and kiss on the cheek.

Hugging her back, I say, "I love you too." I roll my suitcase into the house as my mom drives away.

Once I turn some of the lights on, it hits me that everything looks the same. I don't know why I thought it wouldn't. Walking to my room, I see the bed hasn't been slept in. Seeing the empty space in the closet where Aiden's clothes used to hang, it hits me. I guess he left after all.

I decide to take a bath and rip off my clothes one by one and throw them on the floor. That will be tomorrow's mess. I grab a hair clip off my vanity and pull my hair up, stopping to look at myself in the mirror. My eyes look tired and dark. I know when I was with Jay, I was sleeping. My mental exhaustion is affecting me physically. While the water fills up, I get in. I relax backward and grab my phone. Pings come through as it turns back on. There are quite a few texts from Jay. Some from last night that I ignored and didn't read. I scroll up and skim through the messages. Most of them are him asking me to come back when I left his house yesterday.

Jay: Please come back.

Jay: Answer your phone

Jay: At least let me know if you're safe somewhere?

Jay: I'm not leaving you voicemails because I saw how many you had, and you clearly don't listen to them. I know how much you hate them.

Jay: We can talk this out.

Jay: Let me know when you get home. I'll miss you tonight.

Jay: I know what it looked like. Trust me. I would never have intentionally hurt you. Lindsee means nothing to me. I want nothing to do with her. I should have told you she was coming over. It was stupid of me to not think to do that after what you went through.

Jay: I know our situation isn't normal. What's normal nowadays, though? I'm happy with you, and I hope you felt the same with me. This is the first time I've ever felt this way with someone. I can talk to you about anything. I don't have to worry about being judged. You accept me for who I am, and I accept you for who you are. Married or not.

Jay: Okay, I know the marriage part sounds bad. It's not ideal to meet someone while you're still married. Given what your douchebag ex did to you, I don't think you should worry about how you look. You are selfless, caring, and loveable. I'm glad you took my chair at the bar. I never thought I would meet someone that would make me feel the way you made me feel. Your presence alone comforted me in ways I never would have imagined existed. I was scared as hell to meet someone new because I didn't want to get hurt again. But I met you and here I am. I want you.

My eyes tear up. This is the second time I tear up for Jay. Losing him feels so different than losing Aiden. I don't know if I should write Jay back or not. He has comforted me a lot this past week. Something I would have never expected a guy to do. I don't even know what to say to him.

Me: Hi Jay! I made it home safe. We started this out not knowing where it was going to go. I never expected for it to go in this direction. You deserve someone who is not in the mess I'm in. I wish I wasn't in this situation, and I know ours isn't ideal. You don't deserve to be caught up in my life. I need to figure it out. I will always remember the time we had. You came into my life when I least expected it. Thank you for being the comfort I needed.

I press send and right away I see the three little dots.

Jay: I'm not giving up on us.

A dull pain shoots through my chest after reading his

messages. I never expected us to feel this way about each other in such a short amount of time. As nervous as I am, I don't want to spill my feelings to Jay too much since I don't know what will happen and I don't want to complicate things.

I scroll down and open the messages from Aiden but stop myself from reading them. Not feeling up to reading his right now. I'll text him tomorrow so we can meet up and talk about everything.

CHAPTER EIGHTEEN

I HAVE BEEN AWAKE FOR A FEW HOURS NOW AND HAVEN'T gotten out of bed. It's already the afternoon. I wish my life would fix itself, so I don't have to deal with it. I grab my phone and text Aiden.

> Me: I'm home. Let me know when you can come over and talk?

> Aiden: I'm glad you texted me. Where have you been? I've stopped by the house every day and you weren't home. You weren't at your moms. None of your friends knew where you were.

I roll my eyes and ignore what he's asking.

> Me: When can you come over and talk?

> Aiden: I can be there in a few hours. Are you going to ignore my question?

> Me: You lost the right to know where and who I've been with. I'll see you in a few.

He doesn't reply.

A few hours later, I hear a knock on the door. Is it Aiden? Why didn't he just walk in? I open the door and it's Aiden with a bouquet of flowers. "What are these?" I ask.

"They're for you," he says, handing them to me.

"I don't want them."

"Lilah, I'm trying."

Ignoring the flowers, I turn my back to him and sit on the couch. He walks to the kitchen and starts putting the flowers into a vase.

"Where have you been?" Aiden asks as he sits on the other end of the couch.

"It is none of your business. I asked you to talk so we could start the divorce process." Aiden's eyes go wide.

"What? I'm not signing anything. We can still work this out."

"I don't want to work it out with you. I'm tired and done. There is nothing left in me to work this out."

"Then let me do all the work."

I laugh. "Let you do all the work? You don't even know what the work comprises. There is nothing more left for us. We tried our best. We need to move forward with our lives."

I get a ding on my phone. Aiden looks at my phone and me. I reach over and grab it. It's a message from Jay.

> Jay: I hope you slept well. Can't say I did. My bed was half empty. I was thinking about you and wanted to say good morning.

I smile at my phone, wondering what Jay is doing right now. He's probably sitting at his desk with his laptop open, working away. He was always up before me. I would come down from the room and walk straight to his office to see if he was in there. Nine times out of ten, he was. He would work while I enjoyed my morning coffee outside in the sun. It became a morning routine. I thought about how nice this would be to do every morning. Except I would have to work too. Aiden interrupts my thoughts. "Who is that?"

I put my phone down. "No one."

"If there's no one, why are you smiling like that?"

It's a pleasant change to smile like this. I haven't smiled like this in a while. I used to spend all my time with Aiden. Aiden used to always send me good morning text messages. Even after we lived with each other. He would tell me he missed me on a Monday morning, even though we had been with each other the whole weekend. I can't remember the last time he did it. Why did he stop? Did he stop missing me?

"Aiden, we need to talk about everything."

"Why? You just keep avoiding my questions." He folds his arms and pouts.

"What questions?"

"What questions?" He throws his arms up and allows them to fall back down onto his legs. "I asked you where you've been. I asked you who has you smiling like that."

I have to hold in my laugh. It's funny to see him squirm for a change. "Because those questions have nothing to do with you. Talking about us has everything to do with you and me. So, I've been searching online. We can go the cheapest route and file for divorce on our own. We have little to split, so it should be easy," I say. Aiden walks over to me and grabs my hand and sits right next to me.

"I don't want this to end, and I know I can be better for you, for us. I made a mistake, and it won't happen again."

Ripping my hand away from Aiden's, I ask, "Did you know the girl you slept with?"

"No. How would I have known her? We were in Hawaii. I didn't know anyone there but you."

"Then why did you do that?" Aiden gets up and starts pacing the room.

"I don't know. I was an idiot. I was drunk and tired of always disappointing you and—"

Cutting him off, I say, "Wait! You were tired of disappointing me, so you thought sleeping with someone else would make things better."

"No. I didn't mean it like that."

"It doesn't matter how you meant it. Nothing you say will change anything. Why do I bother asking you? I want a divorce. I want it quick, and I don't want to fight. I deserve that."

"You need time to think about it. I can give you time. All the time you need."

"I don't need time. I need to be free from you so I can have a fresh start. The papers are being filed. They give you a certain amount of time to sign, and if you ignore it, they will grant me the divorce. It's up to you to decide how you want to handle things. We have nothing to fight over, so I'm guessing they will grant it to me easily." I look over at Aiden. He is staring off into space.

"You seem so over me already. I don't understand how you're not more upset."

"I've been hurting for years. Why do you think I was trying to work on our marriage? I felt so lonely even though I wasn't alone. I sat up nights crying myself to sleep while you slept right next to me. That's the worst kind of pain someone can feel while being married. For a while, I have been over it. I was so used to us I didn't know when to call it quits. I didn't even know when I was over it until you cheated. Your actions brought light to everything."

I've never said that out loud before. Feeling it is one thing, but saying it aloud is another. I thought that by working on my marriage, I could stop the pain. But it never stopped. I couldn't come to terms with leaving. Each day I've grown to understand my feelings more, even though I'm still so confused. It's all coming together piece by piece. Having Aiden here is making me realize even more that I've been done long before he cheated. Looking at Aiden right now is making me realize I don't know him at all anymore. I was avoiding those feelings because I didn't want this marriage to end. I didn't want it to fail. Everyone has to fail to grow. This is another steppingstone to growth. Aiden will soon understand that.

Aiden walks over to me and sits back down on the couch and says, "Why didn't you tell me you were hurting?"

"I tried so many times but you only cared about what you cared about. What was I going to do? Wake you up and say, *Hey Aiden, I'm crying. Come comfort me!* I'd been trying to tell you, and you never gave me the time of day."

Why is it that guys see nothing until after we call it quits? It makes it so frustrating. We could have avoided all of this if he would've just listened.

My eyes are drawn to the kitchen as I get up from my couch and walk over there. I see the flowers that Aiden bought in a vase with water. He set it in the middle of the island. He knows I like real flowers as a decoration. It always brightens my day. I watch Aiden stare out the window as I pour myself a glass of wine.

I give him a few minutes as I sit back down on the couch. "I'll let you know when I will have the paperwork."

Aiden turns to me and nods his head before walking out the door. That was typical.

While I finish my wine, I pull Jay's text up. What do I do with him? I decide to text my friend Lia.

> Me: I'm back home. Can you have dinner tonight? Please say yes. I need girl time and I have a lot to tell you.

My phone pings, and it's Lia. I only know it's her because she set her messages to a different tone.

Lia: Ugh, bitch. Yes! You have a lot to tell me. Aiden has been blowing up my phone for the past week. You never texted me back.

Me: Pick me up at 8? Already 3 glasses of wine in.

Lia: I'll be there.

I wrap my arms around my best friend the minute I see her. She's always so dressed up and fancy. Sometimes it makes me feel like a bum. As we head to the restaurant, I'm still a little buzzed, but not as much as before.

"Tell me what's going on," she demands.

Not knowing where to begin, I say, "I'm getting divorced."

"I figured that much."

I tell her everything that happened with Aiden. We pull up to our favorite steak house as she cusses out Aiden left and right. She's more pissed than I was. I can't help but laugh.

"What's so funny?" she asks.

"I've never seen you so heated."

"Why are you not heated?" she asks, clearly confused.

I pause for a minute, because honestly, I'm confused by this question myself. I haven't had the chance to tell her everything about Jay yet.

"More has happened. Let's go inside, and I'll finish telling you."

The soft lighting and peaceful music make a soothing ambience while we walk to our seats. As I open the drink menu, Lia's eyes are on me. Looking up, I ask, "What?"

"Tell me!" she practically squeals.

"I will. Let's order first. I have a good buzz going, and I don't want it to go away." She rolls her eyes at me and starts looking at the menu. Once the waiter takes our order, I look over at Lia. She's anxiously waiting for me to finish telling her. I tell her everything about Jay. She stays silent like my mom did. I'm thinking about what I did was pretty shocking now. But now with her expression and my mom's hesitance, maybe it was more shocking than I thought.

The waiter sets our wine down. "Are you guys ready to order food?"

We both ordered filet mignon and a lobster mac and cheese to share.

Before the waiter leaves, she says, "This is not what I was expecting to hear. But it's so cute." She exaggerates the *so* in a high pitch squeaky voice.

I look up at the waiter, wondering what he thinks she's talking about. He gives me a smile and backs away from our table.

"You think so?" Maybe this wasn't so crazy.

"The story of you and Jay meeting is, but there is a lot of drama surrounding the situation. You're married and what's even more shocking is Jay's ex was the one that Aiden slept with. That intensifies the drama. I would take a chance and go for it and see where it leads," Lia says.

I never asked her what she thinks I should do. That wasn't even why I told her everything. She's my best friend and I tell her everything. She was a little upset that I kept it from her. We tell each other everything right when it happens. We have always been that way.

"I'm not asking for your advice, Lia. I needed to tell you everything."

"Why wouldn't you go for it? Come on, you wasted how many years with Aiden? You have another chance at love. Why wouldn't you take it? People get so scared to go through a divorce thinking they won't find anyone else."

"Well, for one, I'm still married."

"He knows that and still pursued you. So why does that matter?"

Remembering he texted me when Aiden was over at the house, and I forgot to text him back. I pull out my phone and look at the message. That was six hours ago. Now that I'm talking about this out loud, the more embarrassed I get. Especially for him. Why did he continue to pursue me?

If I don't eat something with substance soon, I'm going to black out as I shove a piece of bread in my mouth. I haven't eaten all day and I've been drinking. I look around, trying to see if I see our waiter coming with our food.

Now that our food is here, I'm not as hungry after all the bread. I ask the waiter for another glass of wine. Getting drunk wasn't the plan for tonight, but that seems to be where I'm headed.

My phone pings, and I get another text message from Jay. All he texted was my name. He's definitely trying to get my attention.

CHAPTER NINETEEN

A THROBBING PAIN THUMPS IN MY EYES AS I TRY TO PRY THEM
open. I squint and look around. Lia's room is where I'm at. I
don't remember coming here. Actually, I don't remember much
of last night after our dinner. My head is pounding with every
move I take. Peeling myself off the bed one bone at a time, I
head over to the bathroom and splash some water on my face.
I'm in my clothes I went out in last night. Fuck, I feel like death.
Wine hangovers are the worst. It makes me feel like my brain is
going to pop out of my eye sockets. I work my way over to the
kitchen and find Lia cooking.

"Lia! What the hell happened?" I ask as I slump my ass into
a chair.

Lia turns around and her eyes go wide.

"What?" My hands are holding up my head like it's a
bowling ball. It feels like one. It's so heavy, like my wrists are
going to snap at any second.

"What do you want to know first?" she asks.

My face drops. What the hell did I do? Please don't say I
drunk called Aiden. I grab the Tylenol Lia had waiting for me on

the table. I chug it down. Please revive me. "Just start from the beginning," I say.

"What's the last thing you remember?" She turns a little to the side so she can see me and the food she is cooking.

I try to think. "My mind goes blank about the time we left the restaurant."

"Sounds about right." Lia laughs.

I roll my eyes and put my head down on the table.

"You insisted we go bar hopping. So we went, and you kept taking shots with random people saying, 'I'm free!'"

"What! Free of what?"

"I don't know. I assume from Aiden, but you never really said, and no one asked. They were having fun taking shots with you. I let you be. I figured you needed it or something." She walks over to the coffeepot and pours some into a cup.

"Did I do anything stupid?" I grab the coffee from her and take a sip.

"No, but you started talking about Jay and how much you like him. You kept saying how he was texting you and you haven't texted back because you didn't know what to say. You kept asking people what you should do. At one point, you called him but couldn't make out many words. The only thing I understood is you saying that you needed him. I grabbed your phone and told him we will have to call him back."

Lia comes over and brings me a plate of breakfast. Eggs, bacon, and toast. I give it a disgusting look.

"Eat. It will make you feel better," Lia demands.

I grab my fork and start picking at it. "So, is that all? That doesn't seem terrible?" I pick up a piece of bacon and nip at it. Lia gives another look. Oh, no, what else is there? I chug my coffee. I need to be more awake for this.

"Jay is on his way over here."

I freeze and drop my bacon. "What? Why?"

"You made Jay worry. He was blowing up your phone. I told

him everything was fine, and I could take care of you, but he was more worried because you told him you needed him."

I put my face into my hands. What have I done? I keep embarrassing myself. Can't he see I'm a wreck? I know I told him I was from Utah, but never any specifics. How is he going to find me?

"Lia, how does he know where I'm at? What else did you tell him?" She stays quiet. "Lia!"

"I told him," she says in a hushed voice.

I can't believe her. "I'm already embarrassed and now this. How much more embarrassed can I get? This is terrible. I'm a damn mess."

Lia comes up and takes a seat at the table with her plate full of food. "Lilah, he really likes you. I don't see the harm in giving him a chance. And he seems nice. You deserve that."

Jay is nice. I've never met someone like him. It's not like I had a lot of chances. Aiden and I met when we were so young. I hardly dated.

"Look how much he is proving to you he likes you. Where is Aiden? He says he messed up and wants to work on things, but he's not the one coming over here to see if you're okay. Jay is," Lia says.

"Because I didn't call Aiden. I called Jay. If I had called Aiden, I'm sure it would have been him coming."

"That should tell you something, then. Jay was the one you thought about, not Aiden. People say your true feelings come out when you're drunk. That should mean something."

The second I finished my breakfast, I called Jay, and it went straight to voicemail. Shit, he is coming. I scrolled through my messages and found that he texted me his itinerary. His plane lands in a few hours. I need to shower and get ready. He can't see me like this, especially after I made a fool of myself last night.

I didn't have time to go home. I had to shower and get ready at Lia's. She let me borrow her car to go to the airport to pick Jay up. I'm so nervous and keep fidgeting with my nails. What am I going to say to him? The last thing I told him is that it wasn't our time yet and now I'm drunk calling him, telling him I need him. He must be so confused. I'm even confused. How can I start something with someone else when I don't even know what I'm doing?

I park the car and start heading inside to meet him. There are so many people it's hard to know where he is. As I'm standing there reading all the flights that just landed, someone grabs my hand and pulls me into a hug. It's Jay. I don't even have to look to know. His smell and touch calm me. Anytime I'm with him, it feels like I'm home. His hug alone brings me a peace I never knew I needed.

Why am I being so stubborn? Why don't I give this a chance? My mind is in the way of what my heart is trying to say. Jay releases me a little and looks down at me while I stare up at him. He leans in and kisses my forehead. Closing my eyes, I take in his touch. He releases me again and grabs my hand, and we head out to the parking garage. I don't know what to say or if there is anything to say. Our actions speak for ourselves.

We come up to the car and before I can get in, he leans me against the driver side door and starts kissing me. He kisses me so hard, as if he's yearning for me. I grab a hold of his shirt and pull him closer to me. He pushes his hips into me. I feel him so hard. My body gets warm. I need him. I want him. Trying to catch my breath, I say, "Let's go. I need you." My vagina is aching for him.

Jay is giving me directions to the closest hotel we could find while I drive as fast as I can. Nothing else is being said. Pulling into the parking lot of the Marriot, we walk as fast as we can to the front desk. I'm sure people can see how ridiculous we are being. I don't care. All I care about is Jay. The desk clerk is giving us weird looks. I'm trying so hard to hold my laugh in.

Jay gets the key card, and we walk to the elevator. Please don't let anyone else get on this elevator. The doors open and we walk in. Of course, so does a family with kids.

I don't know what room number we are in. Jay is leading me out of the elevator toward the room. Once we get to the room, Jay opens the door. The second I step in, I kick my shoes off. Jay comes in and I see his boner about to rip out of his pants. Has he had the boner this whole time? Did everyone see it?

He grabs me and pushes me up against the wall, kissing me all over my neck. With one hand, he grabs one of my legs and pulls it up and with his other hand, finding my clit. The rhythm of his fingers makes me shake. An orgasm rips right through me and I moan.

Jay picks me up and I wrap my legs around him. He sets me on the bed. Ripping his shirt off, I run my hands down his body. His muscles are popping out as if he just got done working out. He leans down and kisses me. I can't wait anymore. I undo his belt, zip down his pants, and grab his dick. It's rock hard and pulsing in my hand. I lead his dick to me, and he thrusts so hard into me. It makes us both moan.

He's fucking me so hard I feel like the bed is going to break. We have only been apart a few days, but right now it feels like it's been months. I can feel Jay getting close. I grab his head and kiss him. Jay moans and shakes while he cums. I hold his head in my hands, still kissing him. My head falls back and my chest lifts. Another orgasm ripples through my whole body.

I have no idea when I passed out, but I wake up to Jay's arms wrapped around me. We're both in bed naked. Looking around, I see some light shining through the blinds. We must have fallen asleep after last night. How did we stay asleep for so long? I slept off my hangover. Did he mean what he said in the text that he hadn't been sleeping well without me?

A growl comes from my stomach. Feeling the bed move, I turn my head back and see his brown eyes staring at me. Has he been awake this whole time? "Hi," I say.

He smirks at me. "Hi."

Not sure what to say after my drunk call last night. What does one say after that?

"I missed you," Jay says.

I sit up and walk to the bathroom. I throw some water on my face to wake up. Jay is sitting up after I came back out.

"Lilah what's wrong?" I'm embarrassed to tell him I'm embarrassed. I walk over and sit back down on the bed and wrap the covers over me. Jay is sitting there, confused. I laugh a little and look over at Jay. He raises his eyebrows and stares at me.

Turning my head away from him, I say. "I'm embarrassed to tell you why I'm embarrassed." Laughing again. I lay down and stare at the ceiling.

"What part are you embarrassed about?"

"All of it." My stomach growls again. I get off the bed and find the room service menu. It's about seven in the morning and we slept for almost twelve hours.

"I'm starving. Can we talk after we order food?" Jay shakes his head and grabs the menu.

Grabbing Jay's shirt off the bed, I throw it over my head and let it drape down my body. He looks up at me and smiles. "What?" I ask.

"I miss seeing you in my shirts. Especially when you take them off and leave your smell on them," he says.

"After last night, it's your smell, too."

"It's our smell." That sounds disgusting. But I know what he means.

CHAPTER TWENTY

I'M FINALLY HOME, AND I'M IN CLOTHES THAT FEEL LIKE they've been on me for days. Jay couldn't stay that long. After leaving suddenly, he missed out on some meetings that upset some people. He told them it was a family emergency and couldn't help it.

We had a long talk about how I was feeling after seeing Lindsee and the mess of a life I have going on right now. Jay wants us to date. I told him I couldn't. Not right now. After going back and forth, we made the decision to keep talking as friends and see where it takes us. Lia thinks I'm stupid and that I should pursue this more even though I'm married. She lives so free and wild that nothing phases her.

Right as I open my front door, a smell of food consumes my nostrils. What the hell? I look over toward the kitchen. The lights are off, but I see some sort of light flickering. I turn the corner and look over and see Aiden sitting at the table with a candle-light dinner.

"What are you doing, Aiden?"

He gets up from his chair and pulls my chair out and motions me to sit. "I wanted to make you dinner. Remember, we used to do this all the time."

Flashbacks of us doing this come to mind. We made this a monthly thing. We used to take turns setting up a candlelight dinner and surprise the other person with what we were going to eat. I forgot all about this. It seems like a lifetime ago. Why is he doing this now? I'm way too exhausted to argue with him tonight. I've been in the same clothes for a couple of days. All I wanted to do was shower and go to sleep.

"Aiden. Why now?"

"What do you mean? I told you I was going to try for us, and I remember you used to love doing this."

"It's too late to try now. I'm tired and exhausted. Too exhausted to argue with you right now."

"Lilah, it's not a big deal. We don't have to talk about ourselves or anything. Come and enjoy your dinner."

I'm standing there in silence. I don't even have the energy to talk, anyway. Let alone kick him out. The food does smell amazing. A loud rumble comes from my stomach.

"See? You're hungry. Come. Sit." He motions me to sit down in the chair he has pulled out for me.

Aiden pushes in my chair as I sit down. He lifts the dome cloche and reveals steak and lobster. Now I know he did this on purpose for sure. He knows I love lobster.

"You're telling me you just so happen to make one of my favorite foods so I can have dinner and us not talk?" I raise my eyebrows and stare at him as he sits down in front of me.

"I wanted to bring back what we used to always do. When times were happy."

I dig in. I'm hungrier than I thought. Given my appetite lately has been shit and I shove whatever I see in my mouth when my stomach growls to get it to stop.

A smile rises from Aiden's face. "This means nothing, Aiden. I'm only eating because I'm hungry and too exhausted.

If you didn't bring this over, I would have gone to bed starving."

We started this tradition one night after a long day at work. I came home in tears. Aiden set up the candlelight dinner to cheer me up. The way he surprised me and revealed what he cooked made it even more fun. I wanted to make this a monthly thing that we could both switch up and do.

"What did you do today?" Aiden asks.

"Why?"

"Just trying to start a conversation."

"I was with Lia," I say, shoving a piece of steak into my mouth.

"Why is her car outside?"

I forgot I'm still in Lia's car. She said she wouldn't need it since she had plans with some friends that could give her rides. I took it home with me and she said she'll have someone drop her off to pick it up.

I shrug my shoulders. "She had friends picking her up since I didn't have my car. She said I could take it."

"What were you guys doing for you not to take your car?"

Seeing he hasn't touched his food as I look over at him. His hands are lying on the table, crossed over one another. It looks like he's here to lecture me. "She picked me up. That's none of your business." I don't know why I feel guilty lying to him. He's the one who cheated, and I'm sitting here feeling sorry for him, like I'm the one who is cheating and lying.

Aiden stays quiet. I'm watching him bring the fork up to his mouth. I see sadness in his eyes. Never looking at me. Is he really sorry for what he did? I haven't seen this sadness in his eyes before. Even with the biggest fights we've gotten into, he never looked like this. I look at him again. He looks like he aged more in a couple of weeks. Is he not sleeping?

Stop it Lilah. You deserve better. He cheated on you.

We finish the rest of our dinner in silence, and I head over to the sink to work on the dishes. Taking a step back to get the rest of the dishes off the table, I bump into Aiden.

"Oh. Sorry," I say.

"Why don't you go to bed, and I'll finish cleaning up." Aiden sets more of the dishes into the sink and looks at me.

"Are you sure? I can clean since you cooked."

He grabs my hand and leads me away from the kitchen. "Yes. Go get some sleep. I'll lock up after I'm done."

"I don't think that's a good idea."

"Why?"

"I don't think it's a good idea to leave you here alone while I'm sleeping."

"Lilah, what do you think I'm going to do?"

There are many things I could say but I'm too tired to argue with him. "Okay, just make sure you lock up when you leave." I give him a slight smile and say, "Thank you for dinner." I turn around and head for my bed.

I'm lying in bed checking my phone. Jay texted me, letting me know he got home. All I sent was a smiley face back. Should I tell Jay I had dinner with Aiden? I wonder if he'll get upset. We decided to talk as friends for now, so why should it matter? It's not like I'm with him. But then I got upset when Lindsee was at his house. I keep tossing and turning, deciding if I should tell him or not. Sleep must have taken me over because the next thing I know, I'm waking up with Aiden right next to me.

"Aiden!" I move him with my arms. "Wake up." He turns over and looks at me.

"What?"

I hurry and get out of bed to find my bra. I don't want my boobs bouncing around in front of him.

"What do you mean, what? What are you doing?"

"Sleeping, until you woke me up." He turns his whole body around and looks at me.

"You aren't supposed to be here. Why didn't you go home?"

Aiden gets out of bed with only his boxers on. Oh, great, and his morning wood. That he doesn't seem to care to hide.

"Relax. It's not like we haven't slept in the same bed before." He reaches down and grabs his pants and starts putting them on. He tucks his boner into his pants and zips and buttons them up. Fuck. Why am I looking?

"Do you see something you like?" He winks at me.

"No. Aiden, you should have gone home. It doesn't matter if we slept in the same bed before, it's not the same as it once was. You slept with someone else. I don't want to sleep next to you after that." Turning around, I search for leggings in my dresser. I sleep in short shorts and a tank top and I feel so exposed right now in front of him.

"We had such a great night last night. Why are you acting like this?" I turn around and look at him.

"You think one candlelit dinner is going to make me forget everything? Do you think after everything, I'm only worth one dinner for me to forgive you? Sometimes I question what happened to you. Your thought process isn't the same anymore as it once was. I shouldn't have even eaten dinner with you, but I did. Now you do this and think everything is fine." I shut the door to the bathroom, take my pajama shorts off, and put my leggings on. I can't believe what he is doing. After everything, he thinks that's all he has to do. We never even talked about our marriage over dinner. How did he think I would be over it?

He's still sitting on the bed when I walk back into the room. "Why haven't you left?"

He gets up from the bed. "You know this is my house, too. It's not just yours. If I want to sleep in my bed with my wife, then I will. I see nothing wrong with that."

"You just proved my point. You see nothing wrong with anything you do. Did you see anything wrong when you slept with someone else?"

"If we're going to get past this, you need to get over that."

What the fuck. "There is nothing to get over or get past. We are done. There will never be an us again. It killed me seeing you sleep with another woman. Now you want me to get past it after one dinner? I told you I'm through. We should have been done with each other a long time ago. But we didn't and now the damage is worse than before."

Aiden looks at me, confused. I roll my head back and sigh and let my body fall on the bed. Aiden turns and looks down at me.

"You think we should have ended our marriage sooner?"

"Don't you? Nothing was going good. We were seeing a therapist and only because I wanted it. You didn't even care to work on our marriage. And now you're surprised by all this. I don't get it."

Hearing his footsteps in the distance, I lean up on my elbows and see his back toward me. The front door shuts, and I let out a sigh of relief.

CHAPTER TWENTY-ONE

MY HEAD HASN'T QUIT SPINNING SINCE FINDING AIDEN IN BED with me after he made me dinner. I feel my life hasn't quit spiraling more out of control after finding Aiden in bed with another woman. And then to find out that the other woman is Jay's ex. I can't catch a break and my head keeps rolling around like a bowling ball that doesn't want to hit the pins.

I hate to even think this but getting back to work after these past few days has been a godsend. Getting wrapped up in two men has made it hard for me to adjust. I thought I would come home and have an easy out with Aiden since he's the one who slept with someone else. I was wrong. Never in a million years did I think he thought we would work this out or him trying to work it out. He couldn't work it out when we were married, but when he knows he messed up, he puts forth the effort.

The dinner brought up a lot of memories that I wish we would have kept going. It would have kept our marriage going. Those are the memories I miss the most. Those are the memories I mourn. It's not so much the loss of our marriage, but the memories we had that held us together that made our marriage. I knew we could get that back when we started therapy. If we both worked at it. It was possible to get back to where we were the happiest together. Or at least, I hope.

I miss the Aiden that he used to be. The Aiden that pulled me toward him like a magnet. I couldn't wait to spend every minute with him when we first met. He was the first person I talked to in the morning and the last person I talked to at night. He was so irresistible to me. Every time I wasn't with him, I couldn't wait till the next minute I *could* be with him. I would count down the days and the hours to hear his voice, feel his touch, and see his face glow when he saw me. I don't know how or when everything changed, but it did. Now I have to mourn the loss of a marriage I thought I would be in forever.

Jay swooped in when I needed comfort the most. I know how I feel about him, but I don't know if I should have these feelings. It's a fresh feeling and comfort that I never had with Aiden. It was so quick and unexpected. He doesn't deserve to be dragged into this mess. He wants us to work so badly, but I don't even know if I'm ready to open up again to someone else like that yet. Leaving one comfort for another, I can't tell what's right or what's wrong in this situation. I know I'm to blame too, but I didn't stop even though I knew I should have.

After a long day at work, my eyes keep drooping shut. Every time I try to force my eyes to stay open, I see spots floating around. Trying to catch up on two weeks' worth of work is exhausting.

I decide to start a bath, and I pour some eucalyptus bath salts into the water to help soothe all this tension. While the water runs, I walk into my kitchen to pour a glass of wine for myself.

Steadily stepping into the bathtub to get my body use to the heat, I let out a long sigh. With every inch I make into the water, my tension becomes less. Once I relax my head back, I'm soothed even more. The silence helps put me in a state of ease.

My body jolts from the sound of the doorbell. Just my luck. The second I want to relax, someone is at the door. I sit there debating if I should answer it or not. The bell rings out a second time. *Shit.* Reaching for my robe, I hurry and wrap it around me as tight as possible and hurry out of the bath.

No one is there after I open the door. "Seriously, I got out of the bath for nothing." As I'm about to shut the door, I see wildflowers in a vase on the doorstep. I pick them up and set them on the kitchen counter. These are beautiful. I'm looking around for a card or something to know who they are from. That's weird, I can't find one. The delivery guy should have known who they were from, but he left. I'm not sure which flower company they are from, so I can't call them. After the last encounter with Aiden, I really doubt he sent me flowers.

Chills run through me from getting out of the bath without drying myself off. I gratefully lower myself back into the tub to warm back up and decide to call Jay and thank him. It's been a few days since I've heard from him. I haven't been too good about keeping in touch with him, either. He gets busy too. I bet he's showing me he cares and is thinking about me.

"Hello," Jay answers. He sounds surprised I'm calling.

"Hi. Is this a bad time?" I ask.

"No, just surprised by your call, I guess. I haven't received a lot of responses back from you these past few days."

"I know. I've been busy trying to catch up with work. Thank you for the flowers. I wanted to call and tell you they're beauti—"

"What flowers?" Jay cuts me off before I can finish.

"They were delivered to me about ten minutes ago." *Fuck.* What if they aren't from him? I drop my head to the back wall of the tub, praying he's joking. This is embarrassing if they're not from him.

"Lilah, I wish I had sent flowers for you, but they aren't from me."

"Is this a joke? Are you joking with me?" *Please be joking, please be joking.*

"No. I don't even have your address to send you flowers."

Slapping my forehead, I whisper to myself, "No shit." I'm an idiot. My whole body tenses up. The water feels like it's a thousand degrees hotter. Sweat is dripping from my forehead. We both sit on the phone in silence. I don't know what to say.

"Lilah?"

"Hmmm."

"Who are the flowers from?"

"I don't know anyone who would send me flowers but you." Damn Aiden.

"Are you and Aiden talking?"

"We have to talk. We're still married. I've talked to him about divorce."

"You know what I mean. Is he trying to get back with you? Are you guys trying to make it work?"

I take a big sip of wine. This conversation will not be relaxing. There goes my relaxing night. All because I'm a damn dumbass. I didn't tell him Aiden wanted to work things out when he flew here. He's going to think I'm hiding this from him.

"Your silence confirms my answer," he says.

"No, it's not like that. I promise."

"What is it like, then? I won't do this two-timing shit again. All I want is the truth. I can handle the truth. I know you were still married when we started this, but I thought you were different and someone to trust."

"No, no, no, it's not like that at all. Yes, he's trying to get back with me, but I've told him I'll never get back with him thousands of times."

"Why didn't you tell me?"

"I didn't think there was anything to tell. I don't want to get back with him. I didn't tell you because I didn't want you to worry."

"We agreed to always be truthful with each other, no matter how hard the truth will hurt. We agreed to tell each other everything. I will not stand in the way. You deserve better, but if he is what you want, tell me now."

I'm such a coward. We agreed on that right before he left back home, and that was the same night Aiden had set up the candlelit dinner. Nausea hits me. Am I even any better than Aiden?

"I promise you, I don't want him back. He wants to work things out. That must be what these flowers are for."

"Is there anything else you haven't told me?"

I start from the beginning and tell him everything.

After telling Jay everything, he seems fine. He said he trusted me but would like me to still follow through with what we agreed on earlier. I pull out my phone and text Aiden. I need to find out who sent the flowers.

> **Me: Did you send me flowers?**

> Aiden: Yes, did you like them? They reminded me of the wildflowers we found up in the mountains that you fell in love with. Remember, you pulled some out by the root to replant them in our yard, but by the time we got home, they died. You were so upset. I said I would go buy you some at the store to plant them, but I never did. I thought you could plant these since they are still alive and in water.

I stare at my phone in disbelief. I can't believe he remembers that. When we got home, I found them dead. Aiden never got them for me like he said he would. It made me a little sad that he never followed through, but I moved on. I never got them for myself either. To make it more special, I wanted them to come from him.

As I dry myself off, I catch my reflection in the mirror. I stop and stare at myself. A tear falls down my cheek. Not because of the loss of the memories I once had from a person who was once so special to me, but because I don't even recognize myself anymore. Love is like flowers. You have to nurture the flowers to make them blossom. Just like a marriage, you have to nurture it to make it grow. The second you stop nurturing it, it dies…just like my marriage.

CHAPTER TWENTY-TWO

"HI HONEY, HOW HAVE YOU BEEN?" I STAND UP FROM THE TABLE and wrap my arms around my mom. I inhale her scent of grapefruit and bergamot. She always has on the best perfumes. The second we sit back down, my mom grabs her mimosa that I ordered for her and takes a sip. We're having brunch at a place called Mimosa House.

"I'm okay. I hope you don't mind but I ordered you the mimosa while I was waiting."

"Not at all."

My mom looks over the menu. I got here a little early, so I already know what I want. I always order the same thing, anyway. Avocado toast with a poached egg on top. I don't even know why I looked at the menu.

I glance around at all the people talking and laughing and enjoying themselves. There is a cute couple diagonal from me. The boyfriend keeps reaching over and grabbing his girlfriend's hand. The girlfriend gets this shy look on her face every time he does it. They must be newly dating. I miss that affection. The newly dating phase where everything is so fun and romantic. Jay crosses my mind.

"What are you thinking about?" my mom asks.

"I was looking over at the couple over there." I tilt my head back a little to show where. "They look so cute together." My mom turns a little and looks over her shoulder. She turns back to me with a sad look.

"What's that face for?"

"Are you really, okay? I'm worried about you?"

I sit up a little taller in my seat and grab my mimosa. "Aiden is trying to make things work. He keeps doing things we used to do to bring up memories of our marriage. Or, at least I think that's what he's doing."

"Do you want to work things out with him?"

I shake my head. "But it brings up a lot of memories we had and how much fun we used to have. Back when things were easier. I don't know when or how things got like this between us. People say the seven-year itch is hard, and many marriages don't make it. I never thought we would be one of them. I always thought it was a myth. After seven years, it seems married people would have everything down by then." I spot the waitress coming over and stay quiet.

"Are you ladies ready to order?"

We order our food and another round of mimosas, and the waitress walks away, leaving us to continue our chat.

"Anyway, I never thought I would be in this position," I admit.

"I don't think anyone does. What's going on with that new friend of yours?"

"Jay."

"Yes. You sounded like you liked him when I picked you up from the airport." I haven't told my mom anything after that. She doesn't know he came down here after I acted like a fool at the bars with Lia.

"He wants to make things work between us, but I don't know what to do. I do like him, but I feel weird. I'm still married, and also, jumping into a relationship this quick—" The waitress comes back and sets down our mimosas.

"Thank you," I say with a smile.

My mom picks up the conversation, clearly understanding where I was going with my thoughts. She knows me better than anyone else in the world, even Lia. "At least he understands your situation. It sounded like he did anyway, from what he went through. And he's not judging you. No one is."

I lean back in my chair and start running my fingers around in circles on my mimosa glass. "You're right. I need to finalize my divorce, and then maybe my mind will be a little clearer to decide."

Once I get back home from brunch, I decide to go through a whole pile of mail I've been avoiding. There's a manilla envelope that looks familiar. As I'm opening it. I already know what it is. These are the divorce papers I mailed out to Aiden. He's been staying with his parents. It surprised me he chose to stay with them as opposed to his friends. I don't know how much he's told his family, and my heart hurts thinking about them.

> Me: I mailed you out the divorce papers to your parents' house. They were mailed back to me. Did you mail them back?

> Aiden: Yes, I got them. I mailed them back. I'm not done proving to you we can work this out.

Jesus Christ…not this again.

> Me: Just sign them please. We also need to pack and figure out the living situation.

> Aiden: If you would like, I can move back in. It would be much easier to work on things under the same roof.

> **Me:** Why do you always dance around the subject?

> **Aiden:** Lilah, give me one more chance. I really believe we can make this work.

> **Me:** I can never have a relationship with you. All the trust is gone. I can never sleep with you again let alone have a decent emotional bond with you.

> **Aiden:** You seem so cool and collected over all this. I don't see how you got like this.

> **Me:** I'm done talking about this. You need to sign the papers and discuss the living situation.

After telling Aiden we need to talk about our living situation, I looked around for places for myself. I've been at it all day, but I haven't found anything I like. Everything that could potentially work is out of my price range. There is no way in hell I will move back into a place to share walls with someone. I did that way too much when Aiden and I first moved in together. It was awful having to hear other people at all hours of the day and night.

I remember getting woken up in the middle of the night from a pounding noise coming right above my head. At first, I didn't understand what it was. I kept listening to it and figured out the couple above me was fucking. It was like a routine for them. Three o'clock in the morning rolled around and there goes the pounding. I had to grab my broom and hit it against the ceiling to get them to stop. You would think that would stop them or figure out a way to make the bed not hit the wall, but no, every once in a while, it would happen again.

A call comes through my phone and interrupts my thoughts. I reach over and grab it. It's Lia.

"Hey let's go shopping." She sounds overly happy.

"What's with you being so happy?"

"That's an odd question. Can't people be happy without being questioned why?"

She's right. My mood has been all over the place. I almost feel like saying no to shopping just so I don't ruin her mood.

"Hellooooo! Earth to Lilah. Get your ass up. I want to go shopping. I'll pick you up in twenty, and I won't take no for an answer. Be ready."

Before I can object, I hear a click on the other end of the phone. I roll myself off the couch and walk over to my room. Once I get in there, I sit on the bed, contemplating on what to wear. I'm not in the mood to dress up or even get dressed at all. I'm still in my pajamas from this morning. That's the nice thing about working from home. I can dress and look however I want. Although, I try to get ready most of the time, because if not, I'm in this type of mood. It ruins my whole day if I just bum around.

I grab a pair of black leggings and throw a cute lavender colored sweater on. I walk over to my bathroom and almost scare myself when I look in the mirror. Fuck Lilah, at least look a little more decent during the day, I say to myself. I have mascara all around my eyes. I look like a freaking racoon. My hair is all frizzy and out of place. With little time, I grab a scrunchy and throw my hair up in a loose bun after washing my face and applying a fresh coat of mascara, concealer, and blush. Looking back at myself in the mirror, I'm grateful to look a little more alive.

I hear a honk outside. That must be Lia. I hurry and grab my shoes and purse and run out the door.

After walking through the whole mall, we decide to eat at a brewery. A burger and beer sound good right now. I look over at Lia. She is about to fall off her side of the booth because everything she bought is sitting with her. She said she was in a shopping mood, and by the looks of it, she really was.

After the waiter sets my beer down, I take a huge chug. I love beer. I don't drink it much because it makes me bloated, but when I do, I really enjoy it.

"Lia, why were you in a shopping mood?" I ask and she looks at me with a huge smile.

"I finally got promoted!" she says with a squeal.

"What? Really? The position you have been wanting on?" Lia majored in marketing. She has been working her way up to manage a project she enjoys marketing for.

"Yes! The promotion came with a huge pay increase. I can finally get out of my stupid apartment. That's the other thing I wanted to ask you…" She stops and stays silent.

"What?"

"Since you're single—or soon to be—would you want to move in together? I've always wanted to live with my best friend, but Aiden snatched you up before I could."

My eyes go wide. *Why didn't I think of that?*

"I was looking at places today before you called. I have to figure out the living situation with Aiden. He's not giving me much to go on, so I started looking at places myself in case I decide to move out. I don't want to live anywhere where I have to share walls with people. But I couldn't find anything I liked that didn't share walls and was in my price range. This would solve my problem. Well, both our problems." I laugh. "The only problem is that my lease isn't up for another six months. Either Aiden or I will have to stay in our place for the next six months."

"I'm fine with moving into your place until your lease is up, and then we could find something we both like. But what is going on with Aiden?" Lia gasps. "And Jay. Oh, my god I can't believe I forgot about Jay."

I put my elbows on the table and place my head on my hands. Thinking about telling her everything makes my head hurt. I start by telling her all the things Aiden has been doing to get me back, and then I tell her about the flower incident.

"You did what?" she yells.

"Shhh! Keep your voice down."

The waiter comes by and sets our burgers down on the table. He must know something is going on. He hardly even looks at us. As soon as he places our food down and asks if we need anything else, he practically runs away. I would too, with how loud Lia is.

"Lilah! I can't believe you." She laughs.

I look up at her and give her a dirty look with fry sauce, squeezing out of my burger while I take a bite. "Shut up," I say with my mouth full of food. She keeps laughing, and I throw a fry at her.

"He didn't know your address, so why would you think it was him who sent you the flowers?"

"It was an honest mistake."

Her laugh increases like a fucking hyena. "I don't even know what to say."

"You've said enough." I grab another fry and throw it at her. "Shut up and eat."

"But how could you think they were from him? What did Jay say?"

"I told him everything about how Aiden was trying to get me back. He trusts me when I tell him I don't want Aiden back. We're still talking. I know he wants to see if this could work out, but I don't know what to do."

"Girl, give him a chance. You already fucked him. What more is there to do?"

"Relationships aren't only about fucking."

"Beats me. That's all guys seem good for nowadays with all the sleaze bags around here."

Lia has never been one for relationships. She'll date a guy for a while. Once it gets serious, she ends it. She has been cheated on, so I don't blame her for wanting to protect herself. It's never stopped her from dating, though.

"Hey, take a trip and go visit Jay. You guys are practically doing long distance. Just without the titles. You could go down and surprise him. He deserves that much after everything he's done for you. Especially with your honest mistake about the flower incident." She puts her hands up and does quotation marks when she says honest.

I roll my eyes at her. "You're never going to let this go, are you?"

"Nope. I really like Jay for you. No man would have swooped someone up like that, like he did with you. He sounds like a keeper."

"I guess it isn't a bad idea to go visit him. How about you come with me? Then you can meet him and tell me what you think."

"Why would I go? To listen to you guys bone all day and night? Yeah, it sounds like *so* much fun."

"No. It's not even like that. I mean, yes, we've had sex, but it's not constant like you make it sound. His best friend lives next door to him, too. All four of us could hang out. It will be fun."

She looks at me and moves her eyebrows up and down. "Ohhh, who's this friend?"

"You'll see." I give her a wink.

CHAPTER TWENTY-THREE

I THINK ABOUT SURPRISING JAY AT FIRST, BUT THEN DECIDE against it. He is usually busy with work. It would be better If I found a weekend that he would be around more. I grab my phone and walk over to the couch and lie down. I scroll through my contacts and find his name. When I click on the name, I put the phone against my ear and wait for him to pick up.

"Hey, babe."

Babe? He's never called me that before.

"Hi, are you busy? Do you have a minute to talk?"

"Not busy at all. I just got home, actually. Drinking a beer outside on the new outdoor set we ordered together. Wish you were here to see it."

"Oh nice, did the rest of your furniture come in?"

"Yeah, I need help decorating. Please help me, or else Alex is going to turn this into a man cave. He has his own house, but apparently, he thinks he lives here, too."

I laugh. That's just like him. Makes himself at home wherever he goes.

"Well... I was calling to see what you would think about me coming down there to visit for a weekend?" I anxiously wait for his answer. I know he would never say no, but I still got eager for his answer.

"Nothing would make me happier than to see you, hold you, and kiss you."

"But I invited Lia. Remember my best friend I told you about? I was thinking we could all hang out, Alex included. Would you be okay with that?"

"As long as I can hold you all night long in my bed. Alone."

"Deal. Do you think Alex and Lia will like each other?"

"Well, you know Alex doesn't do relationships."

"Neither does Lia."

"Then I don't think those two will have a problem."

Jay and I end up talking for hours. It feels like no time has passed by the time we hang up. He's so easy to talk to. We both spent time catching each other up about ourselves and what we've been doing. It's nice having this type of conversation with someone. All my conversations have been so tense lately. I decide to book Lia and I flight. I don't want to wait any longer to go see Jay. I screenshot the flight itinerary for Lia and text it to her.

> Me: Be ready...we leave next weekend

She sends back an open mouth emoji, showing how surprised she is. Knowing I'm going to see Jay soon makes me relax. Is this a sign? *A sign of what?* Did Aiden make me tense all the time? I throw the thoughts out of my head. If I keep thinking about this, I won't be able to sleep.

CHAPTER TWENTY-FOUR

A FEW DAYS LATER, LIA AND I ARE WALKING OUT OF THE airport and I'm looking around for Jay's truck, but I don't see it. Out of the corner of my eye, I see someone waving us over. Lia taps my shoulder, and I look over at her.

"Who's that?" She points behind me. I look over and see Alex. I wonder where Jay is.

"That's Alex."

"*That's* Alex? Why didn't you tell me he was cute?" She bumps my shoulder with hers. We walk over to him. "What the hell Lilah? You've been holding out on me."

"I'm sorry getting you laid wasn't the first thing on my mind," I say as Alex approaches me and pulls me into a hug.

"How are you?" he asks.

"Good." I turn to face Lia. "This is Lia. Lia, this is Alex. Jay's best friend."

Lia smiles and says, "Hi," while lifting her right hand to give him a handshake. Alex grabs it and gives it a kiss.

I look over at Lia, and her cheeks are bright red while she tries to hold back her smile. Alex grabs both of our bags and throws them in the back of his cab. Lia climbs in the back seat. I walk up to the front seat and get in. Looking behind my seat, I look at Lia's face. She's literally watching Alex's every move. He walks around his truck and gets in.

I ask Alex, "So, where is Jay?"

"Yeah, where is this mystery man of yours Lilah?" Lia asks.

Alex looks into the rearview mirror. "Was this a complete mystery to you too, then?"

"Yes. Surprised the shit out of me." She chuckles.

"Right! They were being so quiet when I picked them up from the airport…made me worry a bit. I didn't know whether or not Jay was holding her hostage. No one would say a damn word or tell me a damn thing."

"Seriously? Jay would never hold someone hostage," I say.

"Ditto. We tell each other everything and I barely heard anything about it until she came home from her rendezvous," Lia says with a laugh.

I guess *I'm* being ignored now.

"Same here. Jay tells me everything. I know everything about him. Not a damn thing was said to me. Not even when I kept asking what was going on. They wouldn't give me a straight answer. I couldn't believe it. Jay kept something like this from me for an entire week. I was so hurt."

I turn to both of them. "Wow. You guys are being so dramatic."

"Yup. I was pretty hurt, too," Lia agrees.

Okay. I'm still being ignored. I sat and listened to them talk and ignore me the rest of the way to Jay's house. I can't believe how similar they are. It's like two peas in a pod.

I walk into Jay's house, and I'm pulled into a hug right away. I didn't expect Jay to be here. Alex said he got held up at work.

"I missed you," he whispers in my ear.

His whisper gives me goose bumps all over my body. "I missed you too," I admit.

Then here comes Alex, interrupting us with his grand

entrance with our bags. I look back at him and Lia standing in the doorway next to him. "Jay, this is Lia. Lia, this is Jay."

"So you're the mystery man." Lia walks up to Jay and shakes his hand.

"I guess I am," he says with a smile and turns his head and kisses my cheek. "You guys must be hungry. I have some steaks on the grill. Beer is in the fridge. Help yourself to anything."

"Thank you," Lia says.

Alex walks us over to the fridge and pulls out four beers for us all and starts opening them.

"I'll take your bags upstairs." Jay grabs both of our bags and walks upstairs.

Lia and I follow Alex outside to the patio. I take a seat on one chair and Lia does the same next to me. Alex goes over to the grill and checks on the steaks.

Lia turns to me. "Hey, where is the bathroom?"

"I can show you," Alex says.

I sit and stare out at the little pond that is in the back of Jay's house. I felt very nostalgic being back here. A calm feeling overtakes me. Back home, it was so hard for me to feel relaxed. Between Aiden's up and down moods trying to get me back keeps my head spinning.

"Why were you holding out on me Lilah?"

Of course, here comes Alex, interrupting my thoughts. I say to him what I said to Lia. "I'm sorry getting you laid wasn't the first thing on my mind."

Alex takes a seat across the table from me. "Aww come on. That's what you think of me? I'm just trying to get laid? She's cute."

"I'm sure that's all you thought." .

"I mean, it would be nice." He winks.

"What would be nice?" Jay comes out and walks over to the grill. He looks at Alex with a questionable look.

"To sleep with Lia," I say.

Alex chokes on his beer. "No. I never said that."

"Don't mess anything up for me Alex. I'm still trying to make it official with Lilah. You piss Lia off. It might ruin my chances," Jays says as he looks at me and gives me a wink.

I hear Lia walk out of the house and immediately turn my head toward her. She walks over to a chair next to mine and sits down.

We fill the rest of the evening with food, beer, and laughter— the three things everyone should enjoy in their life. I finally feel a strong sense of relief, being back here with Jay. I'm leaving all my troubles behind and focusing on him and the potential we have.

The four of us gather around the fire pit and watch the sunset. It's the perfect end to our evening. Occasionally, Jay leans over and gives me a kiss on the lips. He looks so happy in this moment. I wish I could give this to him all the time. I know he is hurting though, because we haven't made anything official between us yet.

Lia's mouth goes wide with an enormous yawn as I look over at her, and the next second, a yawn comes out of me, too.

"I'm going to head out," Alex says, standing up looking over at us.

"Are you ready to go to bed Lia?" I ask.

"Yeah. I think I'm ready."

We all start getting up, and Jay walks over to the side of the house and grabs the hose and turns the water on. He walks back over to us and sprays the fire with the hose to extinguish it. I stand and watch him while Alex and Lia walk back into the house, saying their goodbyes.

"This was a fun night. I'm glad Alex and Lia are getting along so well," I say to Jay.

"Me too. I'm glad I got to meet her."

I walk over to Jay and wrap my arms around his midsection while we watch the fire go out. Smoke wafts upward from the fire pit, and I turn my head to his chest, covering my face. Jay plant a kiss on the top of my head, and I look up at him just as he kisses me on the lips.

"What the fuck Jay? How many whores are you with now?"

Both of our bodies go stiff to the sound of that voice. We're both still staring at each other as he tightens his hold on me. Footsteps approach from behind us and a sinking feeling swirls in my gut.

"Who are you calling a whore and who the fuck are you?" Lia asks.

I let go of Jay and turn around, spotting none other than Lindsee standing there with her hands on her hips with a smug look on her face. Jay's face looks defeated when I look back at him. I know that face because that's the face I get when Aiden pops in on me out of nowhere.

Alex comes outside scratching his head. "Hey man, I'm sorry. She came barging in as I was trying to leave."

"What are you doing here, Lindsee?" Jay asks, a bite to his tone.

He sounds like exhaustion overcame him the second he turned around and faced her. I hear it in his voice. I see it in his body posture. Seems like neither of us can catch a break with our exes.

"*This* is Lindsee?" Lia asks, pointing at her.

"The one and only," I say.

"What the fuck was Aiden thinking?" She looks over at Jay. "No offense, Jay. But seriously?"

Lindsee is the definition of a bimbo. She has bleached blonde hair with cheap ass extensions clipped in and clothes that look like a toddler could fit into them. Let's not forget the hot pink lipstick she wears. I'm surprised she doesn't have any leopard and stiletto shoes—they seem fitting for her. Oh, wait, that's what she wore when I caught her in bed with Aiden. The last two times I saw her, I never paid much attention to her looks. Now

I'm looking her up and down, and she looks like a cheap escort. I never asked Jay what she did for a living. He has mentioned her always wanting to spend his money on high end brands to make herself appear richer. The way she looks now, I'm guessing she can't afford those high-end brands. Staring at her makes me sick, especially knowing Aiden slept with her when we were married.

"Screw you bitch," she spits out as she turns to Lia and gives her the middle finger. I look over at Lia, and she snorts out a laugh.

"No thanks. You screwed yourself enough in this situation. Good job, by the way," Lia says with a fake smile.

I look back over at Lindsee, and hear a pout come from her mouth. Then she walks over to Jay and reaches for his hand. He flinches and moves back like an animal is about to attack.

"What the hell Jay? You don't have to be scared of me."

"What are you doing here? You need to leave. I have told you repeatedly I want nothing to do with you and to leave me alone. What's it going to take for you to understand that?"

"I just... I really need you. My mom told me she ran into you, and you didn't look so good. She said it looked like you're hurting more than you're willing to let on. I want to be here for you, Jay. I know we can make this work. Everyone deserves a second chance."

Here we go with the second chance bullshit. Why do people think when they cheat, they deserve a second chance? Seriously, it makes no sense.

"You're psychotic. You only started 'needing' me when you found out I was seeing someone else. Like I told your mom, you can't turn a whore into a housewife."

Lindsee looks over at me. "You're seeing her? The whore is her? She's married. She's probably after your money or something."

A big laugh comes out of me. "Unlike yourself, I work for my money. I don't depend on a man to make a living."

"I've seen you parked outside of my house so many times it's creepy. Do I need to get a restraining order on you?" Jay asks. "Also, you entered my house without my knowledge. That's a whole other issue."

"Wow. What a creep," I hear Lia say in the background.

At this point we're all waiting around, waiting to see what Lindsee says next to make a fool out of herself. Alex has taken a seat and is enjoying the show. I don't understand what Jay ever saw in her. He told me she got dumber after they split. Almost as if she was trying too hard to find someone else to latch onto. It's obviously not working.

"What happened to you and Noah? Were his ex-wife, kids, child support, and alimony too much for you to handle?" Jay asks.

"No. He still wants me. He's actually begging for me back. But I don't want him. I want you." She reaches over to grab Jay's hand. I step in front of her and grab his hand so she can't touch it.

"You need to leave," I say.

"No, you need to leave like you did last time I was here."

We're now standing face to face. I reach down slowly and grab the hose from Jay's hand, so she doesn't notice. Once I have it in my hand, I reach up fast, so Lindsee doesn't have time to react, and I start spraying her in the face. She screams and backs up, covering her face with her hands. I stop spraying her and put down the hose. I hear laughter in the background coming from Alex and Lia.

"Oh, my god. How dare you?" Lindsee looks back at both of them, laughing. "I can't believe you, Jay. How can you be with a woman like this?"

"It's a hell of a lot easier than being with a woman that sleeps with her fiancé's best friend."

"You're going to regret this, Jay. Just watch. You will miss me and want me back, and by then it will be too late. This whore can't give you what I can give you." Lindsee's scrawny finger points to me.

"You're right, Lindsee. She can give me better. She already has."

I drop the hose and wrap my arms around Jay's midsection. Lindsee's face looks horrified, and Alex walks over to her and grabs her by the arm.

"I think it's time for you to go."

She allows him to pull her away. Alex looks over at Lia and says, "I'll be back. I have to take out the trash really quick."

Lindsee gasps out an "Ugh!"

All of us start laughing—well, all of us aside from Jay. I look up at him, not letting him go. His face looks defeated. I don't know if it's because of Lindsee, Aiden, or both.

Or maybe even me.

CHAPTER TWENTY-FIVE

THE LAST COUPLE OF DAYS FLEW BY WAY TOO FAST. I WISH I could stay longer but it's our last night here. Alex and Lia went out to a bar. They invited us, but Jay wanted to stay home. He didn't ask me if I wanted to stay with him or not, but I decided to stay. After that night with Lindsee, he's been a little standoffish. We haven't even been intimate except for the kissing, hugs, and small touches here and there. With my short time here, I don't want to make a big deal out of it, but I can sense he's off.

I do like that we have a connection that goes beyond sex. I thought he didn't want to show me all he wants is sex from me. Maybe he's waiting for us to be official? Maybe he thinks I'm still sleeping with Aiden after telling him he's trying to get back with me? All these scenarios have been running through my mind for the past couple of days. I'm not even in the right place to even ask him why. He might call it quits tonight. I was a little hesitant about staying with him alone because of that. I wouldn't blame him. My life is a mess right now. I'm trying to make it right, but Aiden is making it hard.

After pulling my popcorn bag out of the microwave, I close

it. I reach into the cupboard by the fridge and grab a cup to fill it up with ice and water.

"Would you like a drink?" I ask Jay. He's in the living room on the couch with his laptop in his lap. He told me he has some emails to answer really quick and promised it wouldn't take too long.

"Can you grab me a beer?"

"Sure."

"Thanks."

I open the fridge and reach in and grab a beer. Walking over to the couch where Jay is at, I hand him his beer and set my water down on the coffee table. I sit down next to him and start eating the popcorn, trying not to disturb him while he's working, but I'm eager to ask what's been going on.

He stops typing. "What's on your mind?"

He must sense something from me in the same way I'm sensing something from him. "I'm wondering what's on *your* mind?"

I lift my feet off the ground and cross them over each other before turning around to face him. "You've been acting differently since the night Lindsee came over."

"To be honest, it's got me thinking what a big mess we're both in and if we should even continue this."

My heart drops. Goosebumps run across my body. I'm in shock and can't even begin to form the right words. I had a strong feeling this might happen. Now that this conversation is happening, I don't know what to say.

"I'm not saying I don't want this. I really like you, Lilah. We could be great together. We have similar pasts with our exes, and that draws us together more than I imagined it would. I thought we'd both have an easy out with our exes and be able to make this work without it becoming even messier. Lindsee seems to want to come back into my life knowing I've been seeing someone else. She's been out of my life for a while now. I didn't expect her to come back. Like you never expected Aiden to try to work things out with you." Jay reaches over and grabs my hand. "I want to see where this goes with us, but on the other hand, I feel we should wait until stuff cools down on both of our ends. I'm worried our exes might tear us apart before we even begin."

Jay lets go of my hand. Coldness consumes my whole body; it's as if he's pulled all the warmth away from me.

"You don't even know if you want to start something so fast after your marriage. And I understand if you don't. It wouldn't be fair to me if I sit here and wait, and then you end up leaving me hanging. I know you've been trying to pull away from me, and I keep pulling you back to me. Part of this is my fault. I never expected to feel something like this again. Actually, not again. I've never felt this way with someone before. Lindsee never made me feel the way you make me feel."

My chest shakes and tears roll down my cheek. I let out a big breath that I've been holding in. The room seems to spin. I look down at my feet, trying to catch my breath.

"Are you okay?" Jay reaches over and lifts my chin.

"Yes. No. I don't know. I didn't expect any of that to come out of you. I had a feeling something was wrong and this talk would come up before I left. Now that it has, I don't know what to say."

"Be honest with me. That's all I've ever asked of you."

"I just... I..." Ugh. Damn it. I've been thinking about what to say if this came up and now that it has, I don't have the words.

"Everything keeps making my head spin. It's hard to pinpoint what I want, how I feel, and what I should do."

"What do you mean? What *do* you want? Do you want Aiden?"

"No. Not that. I'm divorcing him. There is no question there. I mean if I want to try something with you or not. I like you a lot too. I never expected my feelings to grow so much for you. My heart knew long ago that we were done, and I thought I would be much more hurt over him. My head just kept trying. I don't know if it was out of comfort or what. I'm still confused about that myself. You know how they say to not jump into a relationship right after another one because those rarely work out? They say doing that brings your baggage from one relationship to the other."

"Like a rebound?"

"Umm, yes, kind of like that. But I don't see you as my rebound. I'm worried that if I don't give myself time to heal from my marriage, I'll ruin the chances of this relationship. I'm also worried that if I don't give this a chance, you will move on, and I'll regret not giving you a chance for the rest of my life. It's not fair for you to wait for me. What if I end up not wanting another relationship? I don't know what the future will be or how I'll feel."

The vibration from my phone makes me jump. I pull my phone out and see Aiden's name appear on the screen. "Fuck," I whisper to myself. We're talking about our exes ruining this for us and here comes mine at the worst time possible. I reject the call and put the phone in my pocket. Jay stares at me, probably waiting for me to verify it was my ex calling.

"Was that him?" he asks, confirming my thoughts.

"Yes."

"Do you see what I mean?" Jay shuts his laptop and gets up from the couch.

"Where are you going?"

"To get another beer."

I keep my head down, feeling defeated. I'm so confused. The only person who made me feel myself was Jay, and now he's even confused. The couch dips from Jay's weight as he sits back down with a beer in his hand.

"What do—" A ding comes through my phone and cuts me off. I look up at Jay. He doesn't even turn to look at me, he just sighs. We both know who it is. "Will you give us a little more time?"

Jay turns his head to face me. "How much more?"

"You know I've already filed the divorce papers. Aiden hasn't signed them. I don't know when he's going to. I already told him we need to talk about our living situation. He doesn't respond to that either. Lia is going to move in with me. That will at least keep him out and force him to sign the papers. I want the divorce to be final before I decide about my next move. That will help me gain some clarity, at least I hope. If you don't want to wait, I understand. I'm trying here."

"I know you are. It's hard. One thing after another keeps happening. Let's take this day by day and see what happens and where we end up."

I lean over and hug him. "I can work with that."

Another ping comes through my phone.

Aiden's timing is always so impeccable.

CHAPTER TWENTY-SIX

OUT OF BREATH AND SWEATY, I REACH THE TOP FLOOR OF LIA'S apartment with a pile of flat moving boxes ready to be made up and other supplies in bags hanging off my arms.

I seriously need to work out again. I bang my foot on her door for her to open it just as Lia swings the door open.

"Move!" I take two steps into her apartment and throw the boxes and bags on the floor.

"Geez. You look like hell."

"Shut up. You just had to live on the hundredth floor."

"I didn't want to hear people on top of me. And it's the third floor. This ghetto place doesn't have a hundred floors."

I assume that's why Lia is so fit—she has to climb three flights of stairs multiple times a day.

Lia grabs a box and starts taping the bottom of it shut. "Let's start in the kitchen."

I agreed to help Lia pack so we can get her into my house as soon as possible to help speed things up with Aiden. Her lease isn't up yet. She has a shitty landlord and doesn't care about getting her deposit back, so she decided to move in as soon as she could. This apartment is so small, she doesn't have room for anything. The packing should go fast. Lia goes through her cupboards, throwing food away what she doesn't want.

"How did Aiden take it when you told him I was moving in?" Lia asks.

"He begged and begged for me to forgive him so he could move back in and we could be a couple again."

"He's changing."

"What do you mean?" I question while walking over to the kitchen. I open the cupboards that hold her dishes, trying to decide where to begin.

"He's never begged like that before. I didn't expect him to cheat, either."

"Me neither." I pull my phone out of my pocket and play some music. "What do you think of Alex?"

"He's fun. We had a blast at the bar. I wish you guys would have come with."

Lia and Alex weren't home when Jay and I went to bed. We woke up the next morning and found them both passed out on the couch. Our flight was at seven in the morning, so I woke Lia up at four and she wasn't too happy about it.

"Did you sleep with Alex?"

I didn't ask her about it on the flight home because she slept the entire time, dead to the world from her hangover.

Lia stops what she's doing and turns to me. "Did it look like I slept with him? I was so drunk. I barely remember the flight home." She wraps her arms around her stomach. "Don't remind me. It was awful flying home; I swear I was half hungover and half still intoxicated. Thinking about it makes me sick. I would rather pay a thousand dollars to change my flight than ever do that again."

I laugh and turn around to resume packing.

"What's going on with you and Jay? Things seemed tense when we left for the bar without you guys."

"You could tell? I felt that it was off, too. That's part of the reason I stayed back with him, so we could talk. He thinks both of our exes are going to get in the way of us before it even begins. He's also worried I'll leave him hanging and he'll waste his time waiting for me to decide what I want to do."

"Have you decided what you want to do? The guy likes you, and he doesn't hide it very well."

"I know. I feel bad about the position I'm in. What if I decide to be single or what if I decide to give us a chance and my baggage ruins the relationship? But then if I don't give him a chance, I'm worried I'll regret it."

"You're overthinking it. Just go for it."

Ever since my talk with Jay, I just keep going back and forth about what I should do. I can't decide, and with Aiden popping up nonstop, it's making it even harder. When Jay and I were talking, and Aiden was blowing up my phone, I ended up finding out it was because he planned this whole date night for us to have at home. He decorated the house with candles and rose petals. Then he set up a bed for us in the living room so we could have a sleepover and watch movies all night. We used to do that when we first started dating. Our parents wouldn't let us have sleepovers, even though we were both over eighteen. We were both still living in our childhood homes, so our parents made the rules. Instead, we would stay up all night and watch movies. Our parents would be so mad the next morning. We would tell them it wasn't a sleepover because we never went to sleep. We only got away with it a few times before they put an end to it.

That's when we got our apartment. I was in nursing school and barely ever saw Aiden. Aiden had to work two jobs for us to afford it. It was hard for me to contribute to the bills because of school, but I did what I could with my part-time job; most of that money would go to books and school supplies but Aiden never complained. We were both so tired during that period in our lives. We barely had time for each other. Moving in together assured both of us we would at least see each other every night before we went to bed and we'd see each other every morning. That's what was important to us.

Then, after a while, I never saw Aiden come to bed and never woke up with him next to me. He was always out with his friends and would pass out on the couch when he would come home—his excuse was he didn't want to wake me up. He assumed it was thoughtful of him to do that. I chose to just let it go and stopped fighting him about it. That was yet another reason our marriage started slipping away. We stopped fighting for each other.

After a few days, we finally got Lia's apartment all packed. I had to move things around in my guest bed for her to fit in. Luckily, she doesn't have a lot of stuff. It wasn't hard making room for her. Aiden didn't think she was going to go forward with moving in. He got upset with me. I've tried many times to talk to him about the living situation. He never would give me a straight answer. This was the only solution I could come up with to hopefully make him realize we're not getting back together. I asked him to come over and pick up some of his stuff, and he seemed confused. I can't believe he still doesn't get it.

The sadness on his face the second he walks into the house and sees us moving Lia in is evident. His eyebrows scrunch together, and the corners of his mouth are drawn downwards. I've never seen this face before. It causes everything in me to ache. I know we are both hurting in this situation but there's no other choice. I can't take him back. I will never trust him again. Without trust, there is no relationship.

After Aiden leaves—and surprisingly without much of a

fight—I hear a knock on my bedroom door. Lia cracks it slightly, letting a bit of light in. "Can I come in?"

I sit up on my bed and nod. She goes to the other side of the bed and lies on her back next to me. I lie back down and both of us stare up at the ceiling.

"That was a little intense when Aiden came over," she mumbles.

"I didn't expect him to get this sad over this. Angry? Sure. But I never imagined this much sadness. It seems as if he's more upset over this than when he received the divorce papers." I didn't see his face when he got them. The way he talked about it didn't seem as if he was sad.

"I wonder why that is?"

"I don't know. We are both hurt. Him more than me at this point, I guess. I've been hurting for a while now. I'm coming to terms with it, and he seems like he is just barely grasping the concept that this is over."

"The hurt all over his face almost made me back out of moving in here."

I turn my head toward her. "You better not back out. Especially with all the damn packing you made me do."

Lia sits up and stares down at me. "It wasn't that bad! I don't have much. It's not like I could keep much in that shithole, anyway."

"You're right, but all those stairs. My legs are killing me. Moving is exhausting. I can't imagine moving out of here."

"If Aiden was sad about me moving in, imagine how sad he is going to be when he moves *all* his stuff out."

I throw my hand up and cover my face. "I can't imagine."

We sit in silence for a few minutes, and the more the silence takes over, the more I'm getting into my head and thinking about all the memories we shared. Tears stream down my cheeks. I wish he would done all of this when I was trying so hard to make it work. I tried so hard. At one point, I felt so physically exhausted from how much I was doing. He wouldn't reciprocate anything I was doing. That's when I knew we needed professional help if we were going to fix things.

My hands are still covering my face. I feel movement beside me and Lia says, "Are you crying?"

She must have heard my sniffles from my runny nose. "Yes." I take my hands down and rest them on my stomach, still staring at the ceiling.

"Why are you crying? Are you sad over Aiden?"

Wiping the tears from my face, I turn to my side and stare at her. "Not crying over him, but the things he keeps doing. It keeps bringing up memories. Wonderful memories we had. The memories that made me happy with him. I'm crying over the memories. The memories from a person I once shared so much with. Memories from someone I thought I knew. You're right, he has changed. I would have expected none of this looking back at how we used to be. I miss the person who he used to be. Going to therapy was supposed to get him back to that person. What he is doing now is what I needed for so long. It's just too late. It was probably too late even before he slept with someone else. I was holding on to hope for too long."

Lia says nothing. She listens to me and lets me cry.

I think both my body and mind have reached their breaking points.

CHAPTER TWENTY-SEVEN

THE SOUND OF MY PHONE WAKES ME UP. I TURN OVER AND GRAB it off the nightstand. I must have fallen asleep while crying when Lia was with me. It's six o'clock in the morning, and Jay is calling me this early. The time difference between us is two hours, and he's ahead.

I swipe my thumb to the right and answer his call. "Hey." My voice is all husky from all the crying last night.

"Hi, beautiful. You sound tired."

"I am. Is everything." A yawn breaks through me and inter-rupts my sentence. "Is everything okay? You're calling so early?"

"Oh shit. The time difference wasn't on my mind. I was excited to call you. I didn't realize what time it was for you. Do you want me to call you back?"

"No. It's fine. Why are you so excited to talk to me? You have me intrigued." I sit up a little and rest my head on my head-board. Exhaustion makes it difficult to move much more.

"You sound tired."

"I am. Lia finished moving in last night. There was some stuff I needed to move, and Aiden had to pick up some of his stuff so she could fit hers in here. Making room for her here was something I forgot about. I never go into my guest room. I didn't realize all the stuff we had in there."

"Oh," he says quietly. "So you saw Aiden?"

"Yes. A lot of it was his stuff. I asked him to take it to his parents' house. Why?"

"I guess I didn't think you would still see him since she was moving in."

"That's my plan for him to finally move everything out and sign the papers. I'll probably still see him. He is also still trying to work things out."

"How did things go when he picked his stuff up?"

"He acted surprised that I asked him to pick up some of his stuff. He didn't believe Lia was going to move in. It almost looked like he was finally realizing we were over. There was a sadness in him I'd never seen before. It was weird."

Another yawn broke through me. This time, it makes tears roll down my cheeks. I sit up higher in bed and lean my back into the head frame. I grab my shirt and wipe the tears off my face.

"Are you crying?"

"No. I yawned, and it made tears and my nose run."

"Are you crying over him?"

"No." I debated telling him about last night. I guess I shouldn't have. I'm too tired to get into this with him.

"Anyway. I called to see if you would be okay with me coming out there. There are some days that I have free. I thought I could take a trip and see you."

"Yeah, I'm okay with it. That will be fun," I mumble.

What if he runs into Aiden? What if Aiden pops up at the house unannounced like he's been doing?

"Are you sure? You don't sound too excited."

He must hear the worry in my voice. "I would really enjoy spending time together. I'm just exhausted."

"Okay. I'll send you the flight itinerary once I book the trip."

Now I don't feel tired. My nerves ramp up from him wanting to come visit me. "Okay," I say, not knowing what else to say.

"I'll let you get back to sleep. Call me later," he says.

"I will."

The second I press the red button on my phone to end the call, I jump off my bed and sprint over to Lia's room. Once I reach the door, I swing it wide open and scream, "Lia!"

Her whole body jumps from my scream. She sits up in her bed, wide-eyed, looking at me like I'm about to tell her awful news.

"What? What happened? Is everything okay?"

Out of breath, I walk over to her bed and sit down. "Jay." That's all the words that can come out.

She sits up straighter and grabs my hand. "Is he okay?"

"He wants to come visit me."

"You bitch." She shoves my shoulder so hard I lose my balance and fall off the bed, hitting the side of my ass on the floor.

"What the hell?" I say, standing back up. "Why did you do that?"

"You scared me. You ran in here and yelled my name as if someone died." She leans back and pulls the covers back over her. "Why are you acting crazy because Jay's coming here to see you? Most girls would be happy. But you look like someone ran over your cat."

"What if Aiden sees us? What if we run into each other? What if Aiden pops up here while Jay is here?" I turn my back to the bed and let myself fall onto the mattress.

"Seriously, Lilah."

"What?" I ask.

"I doubt Aiden will come back here after his devastation yesterday. Besides, so what? He's the one who cheated with that gross bimbo."

"Yes, but I know him. If he sees us, he'll try to do something."

"I think they both can hold their own."

"You're not helping."

"I don't know what you're so worried about. It will be fine. Plus, if I'm here, I'll act like he's with me."

"Oh yes, because that will go over so well with Jay." I sit up and pull my legs toward my chest.

"Stop worrying about it. Go back to bed. I'm tired," she lays back down in bed and pulls the cover to her chest.

She's right. I'm worrying too much. Everything will be fine, I say to myself. It has to be.

CHAPTER TWENTY-EIGHT

I'M WALKING THROUGH THE AIRPORT TO PICK UP JAY. IT'S BEEN giving me déjà vu from the first time I picked him up. Except for this time, I have an ache in my stomach from all my worries. My hands are sweating, my shoulders have so much tension in them my neck is hurting. The tension soaring through my body is making me feel like I'm walking funny, but I'm not. At least I don't think I am. I keep trying to tell myself that everything will be fine, there is nothing to worry about. I don't owe Aiden anything, but it still worries me that something will happen that shouldn't. And I can't even think about what will happen.

I wasn't sure if I should tell Jay we should stay in a hotel. He probably would have questioned if I was using him as my rebound since I told him I was done with Aiden. I sit down on a bench near the baggage claim area, waiting for him. My hands keep fidgeting, and I can't sit still. I try to focus on everyone running around trying to catch their flight. Some guy sitting on the bench looks over at me and gets up and walks away. Great, I probably look like I'm on crack.

Jay walks toward me with his bag. I look back over at where I was looking for him and realize that baggage claim wasn't even for his flight. I head over to him. Once I'm in front of him, I reach in for a hug. Jay drops his bag and pulls me in tighter. The tension in my body evaporates. My anxiousness goes away. It's as if he's, my medicine. I had the same feeling when I went to see him with Lia. I thought it was because I was away from my problems. But now I think it's him. It's always been him since the first day I met him. Maybe that's why I never felt that hurt after walking in on Aiden, because he's been around me since then.

Jay reaches up and grabs my chin, forcing me to look at him. He reaches down and kisses me softly. It's different from the other time I picked him up. That felt like he was yearning for me. This feels like. I can't quite describe it. *Love?* No. Not love. Wait. Does he love me? Do I love him?

He releases my chin, and a huge smile crosses his face. "I missed you."

"I missed you more," I say, grabbing his hand. He reaches for his bag with his other hand, and we walk toward the parking lot.

"That's not possible," he says and kisses my forehead.

A little bit later I say, "We're here." I look over at Jay and he's rubbing his eyes. He fell asleep on the way over here.

"Where is, here?"

I look at him, confused. "My house."

He looks at me with scrunched eyebrows. "Lilah, why would I stay here?"

"What do you mean?"

"I don't want to stay at a house you shared with your ex. Your husband. He's not your ex yet."

My stomach drops. My face goes cold as the blood rushes down from my head. I look away from him and stare at my house. Why would I think he would want to stay here? I'm an idiot.

"Hey, it's fine." He reaches over and lays his hand on my leg. "It was a miscommunication. I shouldn't have expected you to find a place for me. I could have looked. For some reason, it didn't cross my mind."

"I'm sorry. Now that you say it like that, I didn't think about it. Well, I did. I guess. I didn't know if you would care or not."

"Oh no, trust me, I care. I don't want to see anything you guys once shared."

I smile and look over at him. "Are you jealous?"

"I like you. So obviously."

My heart is palpitating out of my chest. My cheeks get warm. "How cute. You're jealous."

"How is that cute? It shows my true feelings for you."

"It just is." I lean over and kiss him on the lips.

The enormous mountains that surround Utah intrigue Jay. So, I rented a side-by-side to take a drive up the mountains and enjoy being on the mountain instead of only looking at them. Also wanted him to look down at the entire valley from on top. The fall leaves have changed to their vibrant colors of red, yellow, and burnt orange. I found a private renter online. It was convenient to rent from him because he lives closer to the mountain, and we could take off from his house and go right up.

Jay drives us up the mountain carefully. I told him he didn't need to be that careful and he could enjoy the ATV. He said he was enjoying the scenery and didn't want to miss anything. I think he was trying to be safe with me. I keep catching him smiling every so often, and I'm just happy he's enjoying this.

We reach the top of the mountain and find a parking spot. I open the door and go around the back of the ATV and grab the blanket and pillows I brought for a picnic I planned. I wouldn't tell Jay what I had in the bags I brought, but it was only obvious.

"Can you grab the bags?" I ask.

He shakes his head and reaches for the bags. We walked a few feet away from where we parked.

"This looks like a suitable spot. The ground is flat and there aren't a lot of rocks," he says.

"Okay," I agree.

As I lay the blanket down and place the pillows behind us, I grab the bags from Jay and begin arranging everything. I pull out a charcuterie board from one bag and begin unwrapping it. Some parts of the ride got bumpy; I'm glad nothing fell out. Reaching over to the second bag, I pull out a bottle of champagne and plastic flute glasses I found at the store. I didn't trust bringing glass ones. From the corner of my eye, I see Jay watching me.

"Do you like it?" I ask.

"It's perfect." He scoots closer to me and grabs the champagne bottle to open it. The loud pop echoes through the entire mountain. I hope no one thinks it was a gunshot. I didn't think about how loud it would be and how much it would echo. He pours the champagne while I hold the flutes for him.

The quietness of the mountains is calming. It's a great place to come and recharge. We came around the time the sun would set so we could watch the sunset together. We lay down in each other's arms, taking in the silence while the night sky falls.

I keep contemplating where we go from here or I should say where I go from here. I have someone who wants me, someone that I don't know if I should give myself fully to.

CHAPTER TWENTY-NINE

Lia: Will you go on a double date with me tonight?

Me: With who?

Lia: Your lover boy, who else?

Me: Is that a good idea?

Lia: It's not like this guy will know who you are. We can go somewhere no one will see us or recognize us.

Me: Why can't you go on this date alone?

Lia: This girl at work is setting me up with her cousin. I never met him before. He's been having a hard time dating. If you ask me, he sounds weird.

Me: Why didn't you say no?

> Lia: I tried. She suckered me into it. I started feeling bad about all the dating stories she was telling me about him. My big ass mouth said, "It's probably the girls he's dating. He doesn't sound weird. I would go out on a date with him!"

> Lia: (Face palm) Sooo now she set us up. She came into the office bouncing up and down, so excited to tell me he agreed to go on a date with me. I didn't realize she took it seriously, and I felt too bad to tell her no.

THE SHIT MY BEST FRIEND GETS HERSELF INTO AMAZES ME. I chuckle a little, thinking about the face she made when she found out her coworker set her up. This is Jay's last night here. The weekend flew by in a blink of an eye. We've been enjoying each other's company—even without sex. After the last weekend we spent together, I can see the walls he built for himself. I feel bad I'm part of the reason for those walls. I don't blame him after all he's been through.

> Lia: Do not ignore me!

I stare at Lia's text, wondering what to say. The bathroom door opens up, and Jay comes out in a towel wrapped around his waist with water dripping from his hair down to his chest. Just looking at him, I don't know how I've held myself back. All I can think about is throwing him on the bed and showing him how much I love his body. I've held myself back because I know I need to respect him. But God damn, this makes it hard. Maybe he'll let me try. He's probably playing hard to get.

He stands still as I walk up to him, eying his chest. He's staring at me while I roam my hand up and down his body, seeing how far he'll let me go. I reach his sex lines and make my way down further. The second I reach the towel, it drops to the floor. He grabs my hand, pulling me out of this sexual trance. I look up at Jay. He shakes his head at me.

"You can't have this until I have you all to myself." He bends down and picks up his towel and wraps himself back up. He slowly comes back up and kisses me on the forehead and walks away to this suitcase. I stand, shocked. He is playing hard to get. Another ping comes through my phone, and I look over at the bed and see my phone light up. I turn around and face Jay, staring at my phone. "It's just Lia."

He puts his hands up like I have caught him with something. "I trust you."

If he trusts me, why can't he sleep with me? He doesn't want to get his feelings hurt. I know they already hurt. That's why his walls went up. Another ping comes in. I drop myself back down to the bed and pull up her messages.

> Lia: Come on! I'll do whatever you want. I'll clean the house for an entire month.

> Lia: Don't leave me to do this alone. Tell Jay I'll make it up to him, too.

"What's with all the smiling?" Jay asks.

My smile fades away when I see he is fully clothed. At least I could have eye fucked him while he was naked. "Lia wants to know if we would go on a double date with her. Apparently, she got dragged into this date by a coworker that set it up."

"What's wrong with that?" Jay comes and sits on the bed by me.

Feeling the bed dip in makes me imagine it dipping while he's on top of me. Fuck. I cross my legs. I need to stop. My center is heating up. How long has it been? I haven't had sex in months. This is torture.

"She says the guy is weird and keeps having horror dating experiences. Lia said she would go on a date with him because she felt bad, and her coworker took it seriously. She feels too bad to bail out now."

"That's fine. I don't mind."

"Are you sure it's your last night here?" He leans in and kisses me on the forehead. Something about those foreheads kisses pulls me deeper into him. Does he know this and that's why he keeps doing it?

> Me: Fine. We'll go, but you owe me.

> Lia: Thank you! Thank you! Thank youuuu!

Lia's date set up a reservation at Golden Corral. The cheapest buffet on the planet. The second we pulled up to the address where he told us to meet him, we both want to barf. I heard they cook the chicken on the same table they wash dishes on.

"Hell no. We are not eating here." I turn around and look at Lia in the back seat.

"He was seriously going to take me here for our first date? What the fuck." Lia slams her hand to her forehead. "What do I say?"

"Say you had food poisoning here once and can't eat here ever since then. Where is this guy, anyway?"

Lia looks around the parking lot like she's met the guy before.

"What's so wrong about this place?" Jay questions.

"Jay, the dishwashers literally cook the chicken on the table they wash the dishes on." Lia pretends to gag.

"What is this guy's name?" I look back at Lia. She has a blank stare on her face. "You don't know his name?"

She shrugs her shoulders. "I forgot."

"And you feel bad he wanted to take you to the Golden Corral." I look back over in front of me and see a guy coming our way with a mushroom haircut and huge ass glasses that are about to fall off his nose. His pants are hiked up to his chest. Poor guy, he probably has the biggest wedgie. "Lia, is that him?" I lift my chin up, pointing in his direction.

She moves over to the middle seat and looks in front of her. She looks at me, rolling her eyes. "Seriously, you think that was him?"

I shrug my shoulders. "I don't know. You said he was weird." I look back over in front of me and see he gets into a car and drives away. Well, that wasn't him. "Could you call him and stop wasting more of our time?"

"Okay. Geez. Jay, what got your girl's panties in a bunch?"

Jay looks over at me and rests his hands on my thigh. "She's sexually frustrated."

My mouth drops and my eyes go wide.

"What?" Lia throws her head back and laughs. I look back at her, scrunching my eyebrows, giving her the eye to shut the hell up.

"Trouble in paradise already." She snorts.

"I'm not giving myself up until she gives herself up to me." Jay winks at me.

He just had to go there.

Twenty minutes later, we pulled up into a bar. Supposedly, the guy was supposed to give Lia this bar's address but accidentally gave her Golden Corrals address. I bet Lia's coworker has something to do with where he's taking her. How do you go from taking a girl to Golden Corral to a bar? A bar that has no name. I don't understand the no-name part, but according to the hostess, the owner couldn't ever find a name for it, so they left it blank. All my life I've lived here, and I've never heard of this bar. I'm not sure how they even got a business with no name. How do you search for it? We don't know if the food is good here or not, but anything is better than Golden Corral.

All three of us get seated and order drinks. The vibe here isn't too bad. It's a lot of older people. A live band is playing music. There are a few pool tables to the right of us. There's a patio behind the pool tables that people keep going in and out of.

"Where is this guy of yours?" Jays asks.

"Hopefully he doesn't make it," Lia says with a laugh. She lays her head down on the table.

I pull up the menu and start looking over the food. A guy walks in and looks around while I face the hostess stand. Eyeing the hostess stand, I ask, "Lia, is that him?"

Lia turns around and looks. They make eye contact, and he heads over.

"Hi, are you Lia?" he asks, reaching his hand out to me.

"No, I'm Lilah. This is Lia." I point to Lia. He keeps his hand out and turns to Lia. She smiles and grabs his hand to shake it.

"Hi," she says.

He pulls out a pen and paper and places them on the table. "Can you fill this out for me?"

Jay drops his menu down, eyeing the paper. Both Lia and I stare at each other, questioning what the hell he's doing. She grabs the paper and looks at it. By the look on her face, I can tell it's bad.

"Why?" she asks.

"It's better to know if you meet my standards now rather than later, so we don't waste each other's time."

I hold my hand over my mouth while laughing. Lia hears me and narrows her eyes. I look over at Jay as he watches this all play out in front of him.

Lia places the paper down on the table and pats it like it's his prize procession. "There is no need for this. Let's enjoy a nice dinner and see where this goes."

He is about to protest, but Jay interrupts and reaches his hand over the table to him. "Hi, I'm Jay." The man takes Jay's hand and shakes it.

"I'm Rudy."

Finally, we have a name for him. He doesn't look so bad. He looks like an average guy. Blue eyes, sandy brown hair...there's nothing wrong with his looks. He has a checkered shirt on and straight-legged jeans with black sneakers. It could be worse. His horror dates probably start with his questions. He sounds like he is trying to one and done everyone until he finds who he likes before even getting to know them.

The waiter comes over and asks if we are ready to order. Rudy orders us a round of shots and drinks. He's trying to get this party started—or over—sooner rather than later. No one protests the free shots. The waitress grabs our menus and heads to the bar.

A few awkward minutes pass by and no one is talking. I can tell Lia is uncomfortable. Jay and I both turn our chairs around to face the band. I rest my head on his shoulder and he places yet another kiss on the top of my head. This man is making it hard not to fall for him. It's bad enough we get along like paper and glue. The timing of all this makes everything so hard. I don't want to say I wish I met him sooner because I don't regret getting married to Aiden. I wish I would have met him after Aiden and I divorced, but then, if Aiden never cheated on me, I don't know if I would have left him. His cheating gave me the realization that I was already over him. If that wouldn't have happened, I wouldn't have met Jay. It might have been fate that all this happened as it did.

The waiter comes and places our shots on the table. "Do you guys want to open a tab?"

Jay reaches out to give him his card and says, "This is for me and her."

It sounds a little harsh. We don't offer to pay for Rudy and Lia, but it's supposed to be a date for those two. Lia made us crash it. I look up at Rudy and he doesn't budge. I stop and stare at Lia. She's looking over at him, waiting for him to give out his card. Holy shit, is he not going to pay for his date? Lia reaches into her purse and gives her card to the waitress.

"This is only for me."

This is getting awkward. Jay's head is shaking from the corner of my eye. The next thing I know, Rudy pulls out his card and gives it to the waitress.

"This is for my tab only."

My eyes go wide in disbelief. He's really not going to pay for his date. Oh god, I feel bad for Lia. Maybe it was because she wouldn't fill out the stupid questionnaire he brought.

"Your food should be out soon," the waitress says.

Before she can walk away, Rudy says. "Hey Brandy, can you get us all another round of shots?" He gives her a wink, and she walks away.

What the hell? We haven't even taken the first ones. What was up with that wink? He's already shown way too many red flags in a short amount of time. How long is Lia going to endure this? As if reading my thoughts, Lia stands.

"I'm going to go to the bathroom. Will you join me?" she asks, looking at me.

I nod and give a small pat to Jay's leg, silently letting him know I'll be back. I turn around and we both start heading for the bathroom. The second I walk in, I turn around and face Lia. She slams the bathroom door shut and locks it.

"What the fuck!" she mutters.

Facing Lia, I say, "Now I know why his dates turn out so bad."

"You think? His cousin said nothing about this. She probably doesn't even know. I bet he's the one who put the blame on all his dates." She throws her hands in the air. "And what the fuck is up with his questionnaire?" She huffs out a huge breath. "And he doesn't want to pay for me. Way to make a lady feel deserving." She catches her breath and turns to the mirror and fixes her hair.

"I'm very shocked at everything that's gone down in such a short time."

Lia walks over to me and grabs my hands. "Thank you guys for coming. I don't know what I would have done if it was just me." She stares at something behind me. I turn around and see a small window. "We could jump out the window and leave."

"Jay is out there. We can't leave him."

"Ugh, fine. Let's go."

"Maybe it won't be so bad after he has some alcohol in him. The alcohol might loosen him up a bit."

Lia pulls me out of the bathroom. We walk out hand in hand. "Let's hope."

We get back to the table and find Jay and Rudy talking amongst themselves. They seem a little deep into the conversation because they barely acknowledge we're back. I look over and see both of Rudy's shots are gone—and most of his beer. I picked up my shot to cheer everyone at the table. Lia and Jay grab their shots and we all clink our shot glasses together. All three of us shoot them down. One down, one more to go, plus my beer.

I look over at Lia and she has the second shot in her hand, ready to take it. I grab my other shot, waiting for Jay to pick his up. Round two is done. Rudy is still in conversation with Jay. Mostly Rudy is in the conversation, and Jay is only listening at this point. I look around and see the waitress coming by with our food. Thank God these shots are going to get me buzzed soon.

We are all pretty drunk now after a few hours and a few rounds of shots. Rudy wouldn't stop ordering us shots until we asked the waitress to close our tabs. I've seen people drink, but not this much. He drinks liquor down like water. He rarely pays any attention to Lia the whole night. I'm sure she's happy about that. All of us have moved ourselves over to the pool tables. Rudy and Lia are playing right now. Jay and I have been sitting at a tall round table watching their game. Guys keep eyeing Lia all night. Or maybe they are eyeing us with Rudy. He's so drunk he can barely stand. The waitress already had to cut him off; It's getting a little embarrassing.

Lia finally wins, and Rudy doesn't seem fazed about it. I look up and see a guy heading in our direction. He steps next to Lia and asks if she wants to play a round of pool together. Lia's face lights up so big and bright. I don't know if it's because she's attracted to him or because she can now finally stop interacting with Rudy. We all look over at Rudy and he throws his hands up like he doesn't care. Of course, he doesn't. He sits on the other side of us, babying his beer because the waitress cut him off.

Jay walks over to me and leans in for a kiss. His kiss and the smell of his cologne are doing things to me I never expected. He whispers in my ear, "Don't you wish you could have me? All of me." He bites down on the top of my ear, and I feel his breath on me. Goosebumps run through my body. My vagina pulses for him.

He spreads my legs open wider and stands in between them. He leaves a trail of kisses down my neck. His hand comes up and with one finger, he pulls my shirt down a little, exposing the top of my breasts. He has no care in the world who's around us or watching us. The alcohol is benefiting me. He's so big his whole body hovers over me, covering everything he's doing to me. I look up into his eyes. They're glossed over from all the alcohol. I reach up and grab in between his legs. He's pulsing for me, too. A small moan comes from his mouth. I take his tongue into my mouth and suck.

"Don't you wish I had my mouth on something else?" I say, tugging at his jeans that are holding down his cock. He lays his forehead on mine. I reach up a little further and close my eyes to grab his tongue again.

The next thing I know an icy breeze hit me like a brick of ice. A loud crash echoes in front of me. I open my eyes and look up and I see Aiden and Jay on top of the pool table. Aiden managed to get on top of him. He's straddling Jay on top of his stomach. I get up from the chair and pull at Aiden's shirt. "Aiden stop. What are you doing?"

Aiden looks at me, his eyes glossed over and red. "Who the fuck is this?"

Jay pulls his legs up and wraps them around Aiden's midsection. He pulls him down so quickly I fall from being so close to them. I hear Lia scream in the background. Feeling a touch on my head.

"Lilah, are you okay?" It's Jay's hand on my head. I reach up to touch it. My head pounds. The alcohol isn't helping me here. I can't focus on what's going on. Aiden pulls Jay away from me and swings to punch him in the face. Jay blocks it and swings right back, knocking Aiden to the ground. Jay runs over to me and helps stand me up. I look over Jay's shoulder and Aiden is standing, wiping the blood from his face.

"Who is this Lilah? What the fuck is going on?" Aiden yells.

Jay looks between Aiden and me. "Is this who I think it is?" Jay asks. I can't make out any words. I stand there in silence. "Lilah?" I nod my head. That's all I can do. Jay notices my silence and backs up a little from me. I stare at both of them in front of me. How did my life come to this?

"Lilah!" I hear Aiden yell. His voice is a lot louder this time. He points over to Jay. "Who the fuck is this?"

Lia comes up behind me and stands between Jay and me. "He's with me," she says. I look over at Jay and he backs away even more. He looks at me, waiting for me to answer Aiden's questions.

The look on Jay's face is telling me he wants me to choose

right now. I stand here, confused about what to do. Questioning myself at this moment, why I'm standing here in silence. I don't want Aiden back after what he did. He's the one who cheated on me. So why do I feel so bad? Aiden's face is radiating so much anger I can feel it shooting all around me. Blood is dripping from his face to his shirt.

Jay's shoulders hang low. Both hands clenched into fists. He's done. I can see it. I can feel it. Jay gives me one last look, turns his back toward me, and walks away. Paralysis takes over my legs, stopping me from running after him. Tears stream down my face. I hear the door shut. All I do is look down at the floor. Feeling like a failure. My marriage failed and now my second chance of love is gone. My heart knows who it wants, but my head keeps stopping me. I don't want to hurt anyone's feelings, but the one I want is already hurting.

Aiden is now standing in front of me. The weight of my failure is weighing down my head. I can't bear to look up at him. Chatter surrounds us, making it harder to look around me.

"You're a bitch for making me feel like shit for cheating when you've been banging someone behind my back this whole time," Aiden says.

"Fuck you, Aiden!" I yell. "I let someone walk away from me so you wouldn't get your feelings hurt and you call me a bitch." Pushing Aiden out of my way as I run to the door to stop Jay. I reach the front, looking over to my left and then to my right. He's nowhere in sight. I dial his number as quick as I can. All I hear is ringing. It rings for what feels like a million times and then I hear his voicemail.

CHAPTER THIRTY

"LILAH, GET UP. YOU'VE BEEN MOPING AROUND IN BED FOR TOO long now," Lia says while jumping on top of my bed to wake me up. Because I won't follow her command, she moves off my bed and opens my blinds.

"No. Keep them shut!" I yell.

She walks back over to me and pulls my comforter off my head. "No. Get up."

The light shining through my room burns my eyes like I'm a vampire about to catch on fire from the sunlight. I grab the comforter and pull it back over me.

Lia walks over to me and sits on the side of the bed. "Look, I know you're hurting, but you can't keep sleeping your life away."

Hurt doesn't even describe how I'm feeling. I'm hurt, mad, embarrassed, and ashamed. I let the one person who wanted me walk away. All so I wouldn't hurt Aiden's feelings. For him to turn around and call me a bitch. Why did I even care about his feelings? He never cared for mine.

We were all too drunk to drive that night. Lia called an Uber for us two. We let Aiden and Rudy figure it out on their own. The waitress called Rudy a cab to come pick him up. I didn't even know cabs still existed.

By that time, I was out of it. The adrenaline kicked my drunkenness up by a thousand. I kept asking the Uber driver to take me to the hotel to find Jay. That was even a pain in the ass to get him to do it. We were even paying him for his services, and he kept complaining about how I was too drunk. Finally, Lia talked him into taking us. When we pulled up to the hotel, I jumped out of the car and yelled for Jay repeatedly. I ran up to the room we were staying in and pounded on the door. Lia ran up to me with my purse. I snatched it from her and pulled out the hotel key card. The room was empty when I swung it open, but my stuff was still there. I remember running to the bathroom to look for him. There was nothing. He was gone. Every time I called him it would go straight to voicemail. He blocked me. I felt so defeated. He never even blocked Lindsee. He said it was because he was over her. I knew right then I hurt him more than I imagined.

"At least come downstairs and eat. You're withering away."

I haven't been able to get out of bed or eat. I work from home, so it's been easy to work off my laptop in bed where the sun doesn't shine. That's the one time I get peace from Lia since she works during the day. The second she comes home, she checks on me, offers food, and tries to get me out of bed. A month has passed by since that day at the bar. Everyday hurts more and more when I don't hear from Jay. I finally gave up calling him. I thought about calling Alex, but I'm so embarrassed I can't even bring myself to call him.

Lia pulls my arm. "Please come downstairs. This isn't the way I imagined spending my days living with you."

"Fine." I throw the comforter off my head and stare at her.

"You need sunlight. You're looking like a ghost."

I throw my legs over the bed and walk downstairs with her. She made homemade tomato soup and grilled cheese. The chair I sit on can't even hold me up straight. I slump over like a soggy piece of lettuce.

"Your mom called," Lia says while setting my food down.

"What did she say?" I ask as I throw a piece of grilled cheese in my mouth.

"She wanted to know how you were doing."

I told my mom everything that had happened. It still surprised her that I'm hurt over Jay more than Aiden. She's been trying to take me out. We went out a few times. I'm such a drag to be around. Still am.

"I also texted Aiden." I look up at her. "You know, to see if he signed the papers or not. He never responded."

"I haven't understood what he's doing in a while." I turn back to my grilled cheese and keep picking at it.

A few weeks have passed by, and I started working out again so I could get myself out of this slump. I started feeling disgusting not eating and staying in bed. Lia bugged me so much about getting out of bed. I'm glad she was here; I'd probably still be in bed otherwise. All I can do is work on myself for the better.

I've still had zero contact with Jay. I know I could text Alex or Lia could text him and find out how he is doing. Embarrassment stops me. I don't know if Lia has talked to Alex or not about the situation or if she knows more than she's telling me. She's letting me decide for myself what I want to do, since she has already told me I was an idiot for allowing Jay to walk away.

I have not tried to contact Aiden, either. Every time I think about it, exhaustion consumes me and brings me back down. So I've been avoiding it. We need to get everything done and I know I can't keep avoiding this.

Thirty minutes of walking on the treadmill fly by faster than usual. Since my work keeps me sedentary I have been trying to incorporate walking into my workout routine. Some days are harder than others because I despise cardio. I'd rather walk outside but it's been too cold and gloomy to do that. The weather hasn't helped my mood either. I'm finally in a place where I discipline myself when my motivation is lacking. It's only been a couple of weeks. We'll see how much discipline I have later.

I pull my car door open and get in. Resting a little before I drive off, I decide to text Aiden. I hadn't spoken to him since the night at the bar. Hopefully the serotonin release from my workout will help keep me from the exhaustion I know will wash over me when Aiden and I talk.

> Me: Hey, do you want to come over and talk tonight? Lia won't be home.

> Aiden: Sure. What time?

> Me: Just got done at the gym. Give me an hour.

All Aiden sends back is a thumbs-up emoji. I roll my eyes and sigh while I turn my car on. It could've been worse.

I'm pulling up my leggings and I hear Lia come storming into my room. Frightened by her approach to enter my room with no warning, my back aches from hitting the wall.

"What the fuck? I thought you weren't home?" I say while releasing my hand from my chest like I was holding my heart in from jumping out of my chest.

She storms over and lies on my bed. "My plans changed. I was seeing what you were up to. Have you had dinner? I'm starving! I haven't eaten since the morning."

"Are you on crack? You're going a hundred miles a minute. I

thought you had a date?" As soon as my nerves calm down, I go over to my dresser and grab a T-shirt.

"I did, but I canceled it. After what happened on the last date, I'm too traumatized.

I laugh. "You're traumatized. Imagine me!" I say, pointing to myself.

She leans up on her elbows and looks over at me. "Okay. You have a point. I don't know. Dating is exhausting."

"You're not giving me high hopes here for the dating scene."

I've been out of the dating scene for so long that I never realized how bad it is nowadays. I blame it on technology. It's awful. I don't even know how to use those stupid ass dating apps everyone depends their life on now. It's ridiculous. Once I finally got my ass out of bed Lia and I went out to a bar for drinks and a guy came up to me and asked for my Snapchat. I looked at him in disbelief. He didn't even say hi or ask me my name. He walked straight up to me and only asked me for my Snapchat. Who the hell does that? At first, I thought he was kidding. But he looked at me like I was stupid. Then I knew he wasn't. Who asks for someone's Snapchat before their name? That was such a red flag.

"I told you not to let *you know who* get away."

"Don't remind me." A loud gasp is let out as I fall flat on my back over my bed.

She leans over and looks over at me. "You know…I could call him or I could talk to Alex and get a feel of how he is feeling."

"I go back and forth on what to do and say. The best thing to do right now is to get my divorce completed. I can't keep going back to Jay while still married. Especially now. It's going to show him I'm not serious. He already had doubts. I already feel dumb enough for what all went down that night."

"It's not like you knew what was going to happen. We've

never been to that bar. We don't know anyone who goes to it. I never expected Aiden to be there."

"What you said makes me and the whole situation sound stupid. I should have never pursued someone. Regardless of what Aiden did or not." You would think married people have it all figured out. In reality, we don't. We take our marriage day by day like everyone else in the world that's single or dating. People say adults have everything figured out. I can assure you they don't.

A ping comes buzzing through my ear, and I sit up and scoot myself closer to my nightstand and grab my phone.

Aiden: I'm outside

I read the message, confused. Why didn't he come in or knock? Oh shit, I told him Lia wouldn't be here. "Lia, are you leaving anywhere?"

"No, why?" she asks with a hesitant voice.

"I told Aiden to come over and talk. I told him you wouldn't be here."

She sits up and stares at me. "Why does it matter if I'm here?"

I shrug my shoulders. "He would feel more comfortable if it was only us two. You know how hard it has been to get him to respond to anything."

"Fine. I'll leave," she says and rolls herself off the bed.

I jump up from the bed and race downstairs before he leaves. Right as I get to the front door and open it, Aiden is standing there with his fist up, about to knock.

"Oh. Hi," I say shyly.

Now that he's standing right in front of me, things feel weird and awkward. I move aside and he comes through the door. We both look up at Lia coming down the stairs. She has a smudged look on her face. I know she's not happy I'm making her leave. "She's heading out," I say to Aiden.

He gives me a slight smile and looks away from both of us. Lia is now standing in front of me with raised eyebrows. I pull her into a hug and whisper, "Thanks," into her ear. She smiles back at me.

I turn back over and see Aiden sitting on the couch. I take a deep breath. Here goes nothing, I tell myself.

CHAPTER THIRTY-ONE

UNSURE OF WHAT TO SAY, I WALK TOWARD AIDEN IN THE LIVING room. I never thought it would escalate to this. Our feelings are at an all-time high right now. The tension is soaring through the room. I slide myself onto the couch, leaning my back on the armrest, facing Aiden. Aiden is in the middle of the couch, hunched over, with both of his elbows resting on his knees. His head hanging low looking down at the ground. I don't know how he is feeling. He looks so zoned out. I can't get a reading off him.

Clearing my throat, I say. "You look good."

He turns his head and looks at me with scrunched eyebrows. I shrug my shoulders. I don't know how to bring anything up. We sit here as if we don't know each other. We've known each other better than anyone else. Being married to someone for seven years, it's fitting to know about one another better than anyone else.

He stares at me blankly. "So do you."

"Do you want a drink or anything? We only have wine if you're looking for an alcoholic beverage. Now that Lia is here, that seems to be all we keep in the house."

He's still giving me a blank stare and shakes his head no. This is awkward. "How have you been feeling now about everything?" I ask.

He leans back into the couch and shifts his body a little toward me. "I want to know who that guy was. I'm tired of not getting any answers from you. I understand what I did, and I accept there will no longer be an us. The truth is what I want."

Fidgeting with my fingernails debating if I should tell him the truth. Does he deserve the truth? Do I tell him everything? Down to who Lindsee is? My breathing becomes uneasy. I don't know if it will make it worse. He says he finally came to terms with the fact that there is no longer and us. Maybe the truth won't hurt this any more than it always is.

"For it to make a little sense, answer some questions first?"

He raises his eyebrows.

"Did you know that girl you slept with in Hawaii?" Silence fills the room. Does he think this is going to be a one-way conversation? "If you want me to be honest with you, you have to be honest with me. Let's lay everything out on the table and be done with hiding anything from each other. I don't know when or how we got here, but none of this is helping."

He sits up a little taller and his shoulders relax. "Remember when I took that trip to Vegas for James's bachelor party?"

I shake my head yes. Where is this going?

"We went to a strip club, and I told you about that, and you were okay with it."

He waits for my response. I say, "Yes, and?"

"There was a stripper that invited us to an after-party. It was in a penthouse at the MGM. I think it was her place. Anyway, we all went. Most of us wanted to see a penthouse and were questioning how a stripper could afford that. After looking at that place, I guess strippers in Vegas make bank."

What the fuck? Images of him cheating on me in a penthouse with strippers run through my head. He never told me about this party. Is that why he never told me because he did something? My whole body feels clammy and cold.

"No. No. No. It's not what you're thinking. I promise you, I have done nothing like that." He stutters and clears his voice. "Before Hawaii."

He must have seen my reaction to how quick his response was to my body language.

"We went to the party. Most of the guys were already wasted. I knew it was going to be a shit show because I was babysitting them at that point."

"Aiden! You're killing me. Get to the point."

"Okay. So we get there and there are so many girls. They all looked like strippers or hookers. Yeah, hookers describe them better. It almost looked like an orgy. There were so many men being pleased by these women. Open bottles were everywhere. People were drinking nonstop, and lines of coke were on the tables. I told the guys we were only going to have one drink and get out of there. That's when I met Lindsee. She was a cocktail waitress. She came up to me and asked if I wanted a drink."

Cocktail waitress? I'm surprised she wasn't servicing her body. No one probably wanted that nasty thing. I wonder if Jay knows. Wait? How long ago was this? I try to retract the time Aiden went to Vegas. It was about a year ago. I met Jay a few months ago, and he said then that they had been split up for about six months. Realization hits me. They were still together. Planning their wedding, too. She is such a whore. I'm sure Jay knows she went out of town. Does he know the truth about what she was doing? Why the fuck would she go over there to be a cocktail waitress? Poor Jay. He's been deceived more than me. Aiden interrupts my thoughts.

"Lilah! Are you listening?"

I shake my head, and I turn my attention back to him. "What? What did you say?"

"I said as the night went on, more and more people kept

hooking up. They were too busy to order drinks, so she started talking to me because she had nothing to do."

"What did she say?"

"She was flirting with me and trying to hook up. She would grab my collared shirt to tug me closer to her. I yanked her hands off of me too many times to count. When she saw my ring, she would say she could make me feel better than my wife could ever make me feel."

"What made you not sleep with her then, but in Hawaii you did? And how the hell did you two end up in Hawaii together?" I kind of already know the answer. She was trying to get Jay back, *blah blah blah.* I want to hear what he has to say.

Aiden puts his hands up and says, "I swear to God I did not know she was in Hawaii. Since that night I have not spoken to her. I don't know what got into me in Hawaii. I was drunk and upset and went to another bar to cool down, and I ran into her. She was alone and recognized me. I've tried to replay that night over and over in my head to understand why I did this with her. When I met her in Vegas, I thought she was nasty. I can't come up with a reason I chose to hook up with her in Hawaii. I wasn't thinking. I can't say it was because I was drunk, because I know that isn't an excuse. I was drunk in Vegas, and I chose not to do anything with her."

I get up from the couch and walk toward the kitchen. "How did you turn her down in Vegas?" I reach up into the cupboards and grab a wine glass. Aiden hasn't answered me. Turning back around to see why he stopped talking, and he has his eyes on me. "Keep talking," I say.

"Why do you need wine?"

"Do you not hear the story that is coming out of you?" Looking at him straight in the face. "I need wine."

He shakes his head, agreeing with me, and turns back around. "I walked away from her in Vegas. Half my friends stayed because I couldn't get them out of there. I was sick of babysitting, anyway. A few of the guys and I left, leaving everyone else behind."

This time, with a glass of wine in hand, I sat right back down in the same position I was in. "I hope the guys that left were the married ones." Silence fills the room as I wait for an answer. An answer doesn't come. "It's none of my business to get into that. Why did you think bringing her to our hotel room was a good idea? Didn't she have a hotel room to go to?"

"She said it was an unexpected trip, and she didn't have a room yet," he says with his fingers up in quotations, quoting what she said.

I sigh in frustration. "I guess I'm trying to understand what happened. This isn't like you. Like you said, you walked away from a bad situation in Vegas. I've always trusted you and never expected this from you."

"I don't know. I have tried hundreds of times to figure out what came over me. We were going through a hard time, but I loved you. I still do. That's why it's taken me so long to sign these papers and talk to you about it. I thought if I figured out why and explained it to you, you would still want to work things out," he says, putting his head down into his hands. "I know now that will never happen. That's why I kept trying to win you back and do things that would remind us of our past. Bringing our love back to each other is what I was trying to do. I was selfish for holding onto you. I know you don't deserve what I put you through."

The warmth of the wine rushes down my throat and through my body as I take a sip. The feeling that usually calms me from a good glass of wine never comes. Disappointment hits and I take a bigger sip.

"You know, everything that you were doing to bring our love back is what I needed from you for us to work out. I was getting nothing from you when I kept trying. That's why I resorted to a therapist. I thought that would help you realize what I needed. I was exhausted and couldn't do anymore."

He raises his head and looks at me with sadness in his eyes. "I knew what you needed. I knew what you were doing. I didn't want to put in the work. I was selfish and thought you would never leave me. It was a dick move on my end."

I shake my head, not knowing what to say. All this time, he knew. My vision is getting blurry. Wetness is filling my eyes. I turn away and take a sip of my wine to stop the tears from falling. After a few minutes, I turn back around to face him and say, "The guy you saw at the bar was Lindsee's ex-fiancé."

He lifts his head a little higher. His eyebrows scrunch together so hard it looks like he's going to have an aneurysm. "What the fuck?"

"Yes, I know. I was shocked when I found out, too." I explain everything to him. From the very second I walked out of our hotel room in Hawaii until the day at the bar. I thought I was going to get a lot of heat from him but he sat and listened through it all.

After a few hours of us talking about everything, I scoot a little closer to Aiden. Our thighs are touching. He doesn't move. It doesn't seem to bother him either. It's the comfort of going through this together. I reach over to the coffee table and grab the papers. Slowly bring them back to Aiden, I place them on his legs. He looks down at them like I set down a pile of bricks onto his legs. His body is frozen. He reaches over and grabs a pen that's been lying next to the papers this whole time. His hands are shaking. He slowly goes through and signs all the papers to end this. Once he's done, we both looked up at each other, tears welling up in both of our eyes. A single tear rolls down his cheek. I feel my throat closing. Tears stream down my face as Aiden leans a little closer to me and wraps his arms around me. I bury my face in his chest and we both sit and cry.

We both know this is over. This is really the ending for us.

Everything that we once shared is going to become a memory and not the life we live. I sob from both the memories and the pain. I wrap my arms around him, bringing us even closer together. A whimper comes out of him. The heaviness in my chest makes it harder to breathe. I never wanted him to hurt like this. I never wanted to hurt like this. It pains me to see what a short amount of time can damage seven years.

Our happily ever after is over.

CHAPTER THIRTY-TWO

MY STOMACH IS IN KNOTS AS I STEP ONTO THE PLANE AND GET seated in my assigned seat. The water I drank feels like it's about to come back up. Luckily, my nerves have stopped me from eating or I'd be heaving all over this plane. I do not know what I'm doing, but I keep stepping one foot in front of the other. Out of nowhere, I bought a flight to Texas. It's been a few months since I talked to Jay. I miss him. Trying to push him away was what I thought was best for us both. Maybe I was wrong. He's the first person I think about when I wake up and the last person I think of when I go to bed. I lost my best friend. My other half. He makes me feel whole.

He hasn't attempted to contact me for the past few months, either. I don't blame him. I had a chance at love again and I threw it away.

When I get there, I don't know what to expect. He could be dating someone else. I hope he's not. I understand if he is, though. So many thoughts are running through my head. It's hard to think straight. I lay back and try to fall asleep.

The plane finally lands, and I get up and head out. The bag carrier is in front of me as I walk past it and head out the exit. I only packed a small carry-on. I wasn't sure how this was going to turn out or how long I would be down here. My Uber arrives, and I get in and we head over to Jay's house.

We pull up to the house. "You expecting someone to be home?" The Uber driver asks as I get out of the car. "Are you sure you want me to drop you off here?"

"Yes. I'll be fine. Thank you," I say.

The Uber driver gives me a nod and drives away. My soul is going to shake right out of my body for how nervous I am. I get to the front door and all the lights are off. It doesn't look like he's home. I set my bag down and ring the doorbell. I wait a few minutes and knock. No answer. Jay must not be home. I can't call him. I tried this morning and my number is still blocked. Even if I could call him, that might give him a chance to not come home. As I sit on the porch waiting for him to come home, I pull out my phone and start searching for hotels. I'm not sure what will happen or if he will want me to stay, so I search for hotels in case.

A few hours have gone by and there's still no sign of Jay. I finally decide to call Alex but there's been no lights on at his house all evening either. Maybe they're together or he knows where he is. The phone starts ringing, and Alex picks up. "Hello?"

"Hey, Alex. How have you been?"

"Good. Is everything okay?"

"Umm, yes. I—-" I pause. He's going to think I'm crazy. "Do you know where Jay is? I'm outside his house right now," I say, holding back tears. This is making me emotional. Alex stays quiet. "Look, I understand if you don't like me. I don't like myself either that much. I want to see him, Alex." Tears roll down my cheeks. "I miss him."

"I don't know if I should tell you this. He misses you, I know that. I see it, but he won't admit it. He left for Hawaii a couple of days ago. Don't ask me why Hawaii. He won't be back for another couple of days."

"Do you know where he's staying or where I can find him?" I put Alex on speaker, and I start searching for flights to Honolulu.

"The Marriott," Alex says.

He must be staying in the same hotel when we met. "Thank you, Alex."

"What are you going to do?"

"I'm booking a flight to Hawaii."

"Really?" Oh no, his voice doesn't sound like this is a good idea.

"Is he seeing someone?"

"No. But you hurt him. More than Lindsee. Are you sure you are ready for this?"

"Yes. I'm sure. The only way we won't be together is if he doesn't want to. At least I have to try," I explain. There is a red-eye flight that leaves soon. It's a thousand dollars. I don't hesitate to book it. Around midnight, I should be there.

"I have to go, Alex. There is a red-eye flight that leaves soon. Thank you for letting me know where he is."

"Good luck."

As I walk up to the front desk of the Marriot, nausea hits me in the pit of my stomach. My life was such a mess when I first came here with Jay and now it's a mess again trying to get Jay back.

"Hi, I was wondering if a friend of mine has checked in yet."

"I'm sorry. For the privacy of our guests, we can't give out any information," the front desk clerk says.

Shit. This should have been obvious to me, so I explained what was going on. Thinking she would feel bad for me and give me his room number.

"I'm sorry, ma'am, but we can't give out any information."

Damn it.

"Can you at least let me know if he is staying here so I don't wait around at the wrong hotel?"

She shakes her head. Running my hands through my hair, I walk back outside. This is going to take me all night to find out if he's in this hotel or if he's already in bed.

I glare over toward the ocean as I wait for Alex to pick up my call. The sight and sound of the ocean helps me relax a little.

"Hello," he says in a groggy voice. It's safe to say I woke him up.

"Hey. I'm here and the hotel won't let me know what room he's staying in or if he is even at this hotel. Do you have any other information?"

"No."

"Can you get any more information?"

"What do you want me to do, call him?"

"That would be great."

"Lilah. It's going to look suspicious. Why don't you call him?"

"I can't. He blocked me." Alex stays quiet. "Please."

"I'll call you back," Alex says and hangs up.

I hear music. The farther I walk, the louder it gets. This area looks familiar. I stop and look around to see where the music is coming from. It's the bar I was at when I met Jay. I walk over and go inside and look around. The music is blaring from a live band upstage. I turn my head and look at the same spot we were at when we first met. There is no sight of him here.

I head over to the bar and take a seat. The bartender comes over and asks, "What can I make for you?"

I ask for a shot of tequila. This should help me calm down. I hear someone come out of the bathroom and I look up right away, but it's not Jay. The bartender walks back over to me with my shot in his hand. He sets it down in front of me. "Hey, have you seen a guy around here tonight with dark brown eyes and hair, who has a prominent jaw, average height?" It's worth a shot to ask.

"No, sorry. So many people come in and out. I wouldn't have remembered him anyway." I nod in understanding and give him a slight smile. I pull my card out and watch him ring me up.

The bartender walks back over and hands me back my card. "I thought it would be worth a try to ask," I say. My phone rings. I hurry and pull it out of my bag.

"Hi."

"You owe me," Alex says.

"Why? What did you say?"

"Don't ask. He's at the beach close to his hotel."

He must be at the beach where we went together the first night we met. It's within walking distance of his hotel.

"Thank you. Thank you. I owe you big time." I hang up and take my shot.

As I walk outside, I nearly run into a couple walking in. I finally make it to the beach after what seems like a lifetime. My shoes are in my hand, and I look around but I can't see Jay. I walk a little forward, examining everyone on the beach. A few people are walking on the beach but none of them are him. I walk around and I see someone sitting in the sand, staring out at the ocean. I walk closer, making sure it's him. Once I realize it is, I slow my steps down. I quietly walk up behind him. He must not hear me because he doesn't move. "Jay," I say. His body stiffens. He looks behind him and looks up at me.

"What are you doing here?" His face looks droopy. His eyes look like he hasn't slept in weeks.

"I have something I need to tell you."

"And you came all the way to Hawaii to tell me?" I nod. He turns away from me and looks back toward the ocean. I take a couple more steps closer to him and sit down.

"Jay," I say. He looks over at me and then looks away. My

stomach drops at the sight of him for a moment. I see the hurt in his eyes. Hurt that I caused him. I shouldn't have come down here. I can't stand to see him like this. Me being here is making it worse. My chest hurts. I deserve it. If this is how he felt this whole time, I wouldn't want to talk or see me again. I stand up and walk away. Tears fill my eyes and run down my cheeks.

"Lilah," Jay says. Turning around, I watch him get up from the sand. "What did you have to tell me?" He walks over to me. While wiping away the tears on my face, I glance up at him and he looks down at me.

"I love you." That's all I say. That's all that matters to me right now. I love him and I want him to know it. Regardless if it's too late. At least he knows. I lost my best friend. My other half. When I am with him, I feel complete. I hate myself for taking this long to come to realize that I want him. I want us.

Silence lingers between us as we stand a few inches apart from each other. I can't hear myself breathing. I can't hear the other people around us. The only sound I hear is the water moving up and down the shore. I don't know what to say. I had so much to say, but now that I'm here, I can't even think of what I wanted to say. Jay is looking away from me as I look at him. The hurt in his eyes and silence gives me the answer I need—but didn't want—to hear. I put my head down and turn around. Jay lightly grabs my wrist to stop me from walking away. I turn back around, and I'm instantly wrapped in his arms. I drop my bag down and pull him in tighter. Tears stream down my face as I shake. I'm trying to stay quiet. After hearing my sobs, he grabs my chin and lifts my face to him. He kisses me on both cheeks and whispers, "Do you know how long I've been waiting to hear those words?" He pulls me in closer to him. "I love you, too."

EPILOGUE
ONE YEAR LATER

"STOP FIDGETING," MY MOM SAYS.

"I can't help it. I'm nervous." Lia comes over and hands me a glass. I reach my hand up and take it from her. "What is this?" I look down into the red Solo cup.

"Champagne. Take it or you're going to have a heart attack soon."

Rolling my eyes at her, I take a sip.

"You know champagne makes my face rosy."

"Who cares? You guys are doing this in the dark. No one will see. Plus, Jay would marry you if you looked like a bum. That's how much he loves you."

After my spontaneous trip to win Jay back, we moved in together quickly. When I say quick, I mean quick. After Hawaii, we flew back to my house. Jay rented a U-Haul, and we packed my house up and drove back to his. We didn't want to waste another minute being apart. I was worried about what my mom and Lia would think, but they were excited for me. They both said that nothing we have done has been by the norm and that makes us. What is normal these days anyways?

Lia took over my lease since it wasn't up yet. She didn't

mind and could afford it after her promotion. Our living together didn't last long, which made her a little upset. But I told her she was the one that kept telling me to give Jay a chance, so it was partially her fault. I begged her to move out there with me, but with her new position, she didn't want to give it up yet.

"Okay, I'm all done," my mom says.

I'm nervous about seeing what I look like. I told my mom I wanted nothing fancy. The wedding should be simple. She and Lia insisted on doing my hair and makeup.

One month before our first anniversary, Jay proposed to me. He wanted to propose on our one-year mark, but he also decided that he wanted to set our wedding date on that day instead. Jay was willing to marry me the second we made it official. I told him no. Before we made that commitment, I wanted us to live together. I told him to at least give us a year to see how things went. Since I said no to getting married right away, I couldn't say no to him asking me to move in. I had to compromise somewhere.

In the hotel room we set up as a bride's suite, I get up and walk over to the bathroom. The three of us girls have been staying in this room. Jay and Alex got their room on a different floor. They made us do that so we would have fewer chances of running into each other on the day of the wedding. Jay and I kept rolling our eyes every time we heard something new they planned. We didn't want a big wedding. We both have been there and done that. All we wanted was for our closest friends to be with us, including my mom. Alex even got ordained to officiate our wedding.

When Jay and I flew back to Utah to pack up my stuff, I finally had my mom come over and meet him. After I told her what I was doing, she looked at us like we were crazy. But she trusted my decision. She has always had trust in me. That's what made us close as mother and daughter. Her trust in me gave us less to fight about. Some mothers and daughters bicker all the time because the mom never trusts her daughter and the decisions she makes, and that drives the relationship away. We took our time packing everything. Which was good because it gave my mom a chance to get to know Jay. She was grateful for that. She spent a lot of time with us, and I could see her worry ease off a little each day.

I was trying to throw as much away as possible without leaving Lia with nothing. Lia left her furniture at her old apartment. It was a blessing that she brought little furniture with her. It's hard to combine households. I didn't want to do that with her and then with Jay. Aiden took little with him when he moved all his stuff out. He said he wanted a fresh start.

I haven't seen or heard from Aiden much. He came and moved his stuff out a few weeks after he signed the papers. He was hurting more than he let on and needed some time after that night. We ended up being civil with each other. Holding no one responsible for losing our marriage. He was still a little devastated after moving everything out.

My smile spreads across my face as I look at myself in the mirror. I am so beautiful. My makeup looks natural, surprisingly, even though they spent hours on it. My hair is down and curled in big, beautiful waves. It looks like me. Nothing is over the top.

"How do you like it?" Lia asks walking through the bathroom.

I turn to her and give her a hug. "I love it. You guys didn't make me look like a pinup model."

Laughter comes through the background. "We told you we wouldn't make you look too extravagant!" my mom yells.

Lia, on the other hand, went all out. She looks like she is the one getting married and not me. She gave herself a smokey eye look with a nude lip.

My mom comes into the bathroom with our dresses in hand. We picked out dresses together before flying out to Hawaii. Lia and my mom both flew down to Texas, and we went dress shopping. All three of us found cute summer dresses to wear. Mine is a white dress with thin straps that cut down to my chest in the shape of a V. It clings to my curves perfectly. Not too tight and not too loose. It hangs a little past my knees from the back and opens in the front with a slit coming up to my thigh.

"Are you girls ready to put on our dresses?"

Grabbing my dress from my mom, I say. "You guys will have to help me get into this, so I don't get makeup on it."

"Let's do it outside the bathroom. Where we have more room." My mom leads the way out to the bathroom. I walk over to the dresser and take another sip of my champagne.

All three of us are examining our new dresses in the mirror.

"I don't know why we have to ruin our dresses with sandals," Lia says.

"The plan was to walk on the beach barefoot. You try wearing heels in the sand. You'll sink right down. We're walking down there, anyway. Our feet will hurt by the time we get to the beach. But you can wear whatever you want," I say, facing Lia.

She rolls her eyes at me. Jay and I wanted our wedding to be as simple as possible. Including our attire. Jay and Alex are wearing light tan shorts with simple white T-shirts. They are also wearing sandals to go with their outfits, but we wanted everyone to be barefoot on the beach.

Anxiousness fills me as we get closer to the beach. Lia made sure that the boys were at the beach before we walked down. We all stop once we hit the sand. I look straight ahead, closer to the water, and see Jay and Alex. They look like two small people, making it hard to recognize who they are. I'm not worried about Jay seeing me. I didn't even care for him to see me before the wedding. This was all my mom and Lia's doing.

My mom turns to me and wraps her arms around me. "I love you, sweetie," she says.

I reciprocate the hug and tell her, "Thank you for always

trusting my decisions, even though they have been questionable this past year."

"You have one life to live. I never want to hold you back on anything you wish to do. I will always be here for you. Even when I question your decisions." We both pull away and look at each other and smile. She gives me a wink before stepping back and letting me go.

Within a matter of seconds, Lia pulls me into an enormous hug and squeals. "I can't believe you're finally doing this. You could have let Jay sweep you off your feet the first time you guys met in Hawaii and saved yourself all the shit you put yourself through. It would have saved you a lot of trouble. You both deserve this, though. Finally."

I laugh, finally feeling weightless. "Thanks for your heartfelt speech."

Lia releases me. "Anytime. That's what I'm here for."

My mom reaches up and grabs Lia's hand. "Ready?" Lia nods and takes my mom's hand into hers. They both turn their backs on me and walk toward the ocean.

I'm standing on top of the sand barefoot, waiting anxiously to walk down. I lift my wrist and look at my watch. Only ten more minutes until midnight hits. My mom and Lia finally made it down. Now it's my turn. The time could not be moving any slower. My heart is racing, waiting until I take the next steps down. I'm not sure why Jay and I chose midnight to get married. The first time we came to this beach was around two in the morning. We both wanted it to be very intimate and midnight seemed like the perfect time with no one around. My foot sinks into the sand as I take my first step. Each step I take my heart rate increases. The sound of the waves hitting the shore and flowing back up is the perfect harmony for our wedding song.

After we say our vows, Alex and Lia pass around champagne. My mom orders two special flutes for Jay and I that read *Ever After*. Our names are on each of them—it makes me swoon when I see my new last name on the glass. We all sit around passing around stories and laughing. Most of the stories that come from our three guests are about how Jay and I met and what each one thought about the whole thing. They all thought we were crazy, and nothing surprises them at this point.

I reach over to Jay and link my arm with his as I rest my head against his shoulder. Jay plants a kiss on top of my head, and I look around. I can't help but laugh along about everything that happened to get us to this point. Our path was anything but normal, but I wouldn't change any of it.

It's perfect. It's us. Our ever after.

ABOUT THE AUTHOR

Mia enjoys spending time with her husband and two spoiled dogs. When she's not home reading, writing, or binge-watching shows, she's traveling the world and spends every chance she can get outdoors in the summertime.

Website:
https://www.authormiaskye.com/
Goodreads:
https://www.goodreads.com/author/show/22332113.Mia_Skye
Facebook:
https://www.facebook.com/authormiaskye/
Instagram:
https://www.instagram.com/author.miaskye
TikTok:
https://www.tiktok.com/@authormiaskye

Made in the USA
Middletown, DE
24 April 2023

29065740R00135